ORANGE LILIES
ARE EVERYWHERE

Best Wishes

D A Martin

BY
D. A. MARTIN

Orange Lilies Are Everywhere

Copyright © 2019 by D. A. Martin. All rights reserved.

Published in the United States of America

ISBN 978-1-7341698-1-2 (Paperback)
ISBN 978-1-7341698-0-5 (Ebook)

DEDICATION

This book is dedicated to my friends who encouraged me to tell this story. My gratitude to Billie Davis and Carolyn Wood, who spent many hours helping me polish the manuscript.

PROLOGUE

"I'll show them!" thirteen-year-old William muttered as he stomped into the barn.

His world was dark and hopeless. Things began going sour for him when his principal put him in detention after he told his teacher to go screw herself. By the time he arrived home that afternoon, the principal had already called his parents and they grounded him without even listening to his side of the story.

He went into the barn and picked up a ten-gallon can of gasoline. "Screw you all! I'll make you pay for treating me like crap!" he yelled as he walked through the yard with the gasoline can. Small beads of sweat appeared on his forehead and he breathed heavily as he carried the gasoline can up the front porch steps. His mind was a jumble of thoughts, but he knew he was going to make them pay.

William opened the front door and walked into the living room. He could hear his parents, brother, and sister talking in the kitchen at the back of the house. A smile spread across his face as he poured the gasoline on the couch and curtains. He walked into the middle of the room and pulled a lighter out of his pocket. He looked around the room and was satisfied with how much gas he had used. His thumb slowly slid over the lighter's wheel. When the flame appeared, he touched it to the edge of the gasoline trail. The gasoline ignited with a whooshing sound. William watched the flames as they grew, following the trail of gasoline. The curtains ignited and fierce flames climbed to the ceiling. He heard his mother scream and he laughed.

Suddenly, he was grabbed from behind and spun around. He saw his father's furious face for an instant before his father's huge fist hit his jaw. The punch dazed him for a few seconds. Those few seconds gave his father time to grab his arm and drag him through the dining room, kitchen, and out through the back door as the flames rapidly spread through the old house. Before William could break free, his father hit him again - hard. The punch temporarily knocked him out and he fell to the ground. When he woke up a few moments later, he was lying face down on the ground. "Leave me alone!" William cried. He struggled to get up, but his father held him down with his foot as he used his belt to tie William's hands together. "You damn fool! What the hell were you thinking?" his father sputtered. He jerked William to his feet, dragged him to the truck, and shoved him into the passenger seat. Through the black smoke, William could see his mother and sister standing in the yard crying as they watched the house burn. His brother was trying to douse the flames with water from a garden hose, but the small stream of water was useless against the growing fire. Flames had already engulfed the entire house and it would be a total loss. Smiling, William thought, *I showed them*. His father started the engine and stomped on the gas pedal. Although his wrists hurt, William sat in the truck quietly because he knew his father was taking him back to the hospital.

The first time he was taken to the hospital was when he hit his brother in the stomach with a baseball bat, causing his brother's spleen to rupture. The doctor put him in the psych ward for a week while the doctors ran psychological tests and started him on medication. His doctor had said that he would have to take the medicine for the rest of his life, but William didn't believe him. A month after he got out of the hospital, he quit taking the medicine. Then, a few months after he stopped the medicine, he had to go back into the hospital because he had thrown a pot of boiling water at his mother. He tried to tell the doctor that his mother just wouldn't listen and being off the pills didn't have anything to do with it. She was making spaghetti for dinner again and he had told her he didn't want spaghetti.

After several days of trying to get the doctor to see things his way, William realized that he wasn't going to get out of the hospital unless he played along with what the doctor wanted. He convinced the doctor that he did believe he needed the medicine and promised he would take it. The doctor sent him home with the same pills that he had given him before. He hated how the pills made him feel. He had trouble thinking, his hands shook, and he felt like a zombie while he was on them.

William flushed those pills down the toilet as soon as he got home. It only took a short time of not taking the pills for his emotions to come roaring back. He bounced from being gloriously happy to the depths of despair. Unfortunately, today the two extremes had merged.

On the ride to the hospital, William tried to think about what he was going to tell the doctor, but he couldn't keep his thoughts straight. He knew that the doctor would question him about how he was feeling and what he had been thinking when he started the fire. He would have to say that he felt bad for what he had done and really hadn't meant to do any serious damage. In William's opinion, the doctor was stupid, just like everyone else. He knew he was smarter than all of them. He would give the doctor his, "I'm so sorry for what I did," story and everything would be fine.

The truck screeched to a stop in front of the emergency room door. His father reached across William and locked the passenger door. "You sit here and keep your damn mouth shut!" his father hissed. Then he went into the hospital. He was gone quite some time when it finally occurred to William to wonder why his father hadn't taken him into the hospital. He couldn't figure that out but he wasn't worried. Even if he had to stay in the hospital for a few days, the doctor would just give him more pills and send him home. He knew he was going to throw them away, too. He was surprised when he saw the doctor run out with his father. His father unlocked the door and jerked it open. The doctor stepped up to the truck and shoved a needle into his arm. William's last thought, as he was losing consciousness, was, *What the hell is happening now?*

When William woke from a drugged sleep a few hours later, he realized that he was strapped down on a bed. There was nothing else in the room and wire mesh covered the window. He wore nothing but a hospital gown and his underwear. *Great, they put me in the psych ward again.* He screamed as loudly as he could, "Let me out of here!"

A nurse unlocked the door, entered the room, and removed the restraints. She told him to get dressed and stay in the room. A short while after he was dressed, a police officer appeared in the doorway, walked over to him, and said, "Hands behind your back." William did as he was told and thought that this must be some kind of shock therapy to teach him a lesson, so he played along. The officer put handcuffs on his wrists and held his arm as he steered him down the hall. *Where's Dad? Where's the doctor? Where's this idiot taking me?* He was confused and still a little groggy, but he knew that now was the time to be cooperative so that all of them would be fooled into thinking that he was really sorry for burning down the house. His jaw was throbbing where his father had hit him, and the handcuffs were cutting into his wrists as they walked out of the hospital. The police officer put him in a patrol car and drove away from the hospital. William demanded to know where he was being taken, but the officer didn't answer him. The patrol car stopped in front of the courthouse. The officer led him into a room where his parents sat at a table in front of a judge. He had known there would be trouble because he set the house on fire, but this? He hadn't expected to land in front of a judge.

His mother cried while his father testified that he had deliberately set the house on fire. His father handed the judge a piece of paper from the doctor. The judge read the paper and made some notes in the margins as his father continued to talk. "We've tried to keep him on his medicine but he throws it away. He's already thrown a pot of boiling water at his mother, and he beat his brother so badly that his brother had to have surgery. We can't control him. He's crazy and just plain evil! If something isn't done, he's going to kill someone the next time he goes off his medicine." William seethed. *How dare he make me look like a monster? I was provoked into doing those things!*

William tried to defend himself, "Anyone would have done the same thing if they had to put up with stupid people like them." The judge told him to be quiet but he screamed at the judge, "Who're you going to believe--that stupid bastard or me?" The officer moved over and put his hand on William's shoulders. He tried to squirm away from the officer's grasp, but the officer held tight.

The judge told William's parents that he was sorry for their situation and fully understood that they had not come to this point easily. He looked at William and said, "Son, I have no choice but to remand you to a state juvenile detention facility where you will be forced to take your medication. If you are as smart as you think you are, you won't cause any trouble while you're in there." The judge then declared that he should stay in the detention facility until his eighteenth birthday or until doctors determined it was safe to send him home. His parents stood up and left the room without looking at or speaking to him. William screamed, "Someone help me!" as the officer dragged him away. William stayed in the detention center until he was eighteen years old.

COLLEGE

CHAPTER 1

The small third-floor dorm room in Case Hall was a shock when Elizabeth first saw it on move-in day. The new freshman dorm, Telford Hall, had not been completed on time, and the university was forced to put three girls in each small room. She stood in the hallway, looked into the room, and realized that the two girls who were already in there had planned to be roommates. They had matching bedspreads and their belongings took up most of the space in the room. She felt like the odd girl out. She had looked forward to going to college and being on her own. When she saw the two girls, it immediately brought on a flood of doubts. Her mother gave her a slight push into the room. Elizabeth put on her best smile and introduced herself as she timidly entered the room. "Hi, I'm Elizabeth".

She looked over the small room and wondered where she could put her possessions. There were two desks at each end of the left wall, but they were already covered with her new roommates' pictures and books. A bunk bed and a twin bed sat between the desks with only three feet of floor space separating the beds. Obviously, she was going to have to use the top bunk because the two beds on the floor were already made up. Two wooden closets were attached to the concrete wall opposite the desks. Each closet had a drawer at the bottom, but they already filled. A small sink and mirror were nestled between the closets, but there was no room for her things there either.

No appliances such as refrigerators, TVs, or hot plates were allowed in the rooms. Freshmen were not even allowed to have a phone in their rooms, and the two pay phones on the floor were at the end of the hallway. The small room would have been crowded with just two girls, but with three, it seemed like an impossible situation.

Vivian and Maria got up from their beds and smiled at Elizabeth and her parents when they came into the room. Both girls introduced themselves and enthusiastically welcomed Elizabeth to her new home. Vivian went to her closet, pulled out a burgundy bedspread, and laid it on the top bunk. "My mother bought them for us as a 'going to college' present. Burgundy and white are Eastern's colors and she thought decorating our room in school colors would be cute. You don't have to use it if you don't want to."

Maria interrupted, "Wow, you look just like Natalie Wood!"

Maria's comment caused Elizabeth to blush. Nevertheless, she was relieved that they were welcoming her instead of freezing her out. "I love the idea of having matching bedspreads. They'll make our room look cool. Your mother was sweet to buy them. How did she know to buy three? I thought we would only have one roommate."

Maria said, "One of our friends is a dorm counselor and she knew they were gonna stack us in here like sardines until Telford opens next semester. Vivian and I are gonna move to Telford next semester. Those rooms have phones and private bathrooms. We can make do until then, but it's gonna be tight."

Maria tried to push her clothes to the side of the closet. Even after doing this, there was only about a foot of space left for Elizabeth's clothes. Elizabeth knew there was no way the closet space was enough for even part of her clothes. Trying to appear grateful, Elizabeth said, "Thank you for the offer. Putting all of our clothes in such a small space won't work. Our clothes will be a wrinkled mess." She struggled to hold back tears and like a little child, she looked to her father for an answer. He was always able to figure things out faster than anyone she knew. He smiled, winked, and said, "I'll go find a clothes rack and a small three drawer dresser." While her parents were gone, she sorted through her boxes to separate out the essentials that she would be able to keep. The end result was that most of the boxes were filled to go back home with her parents.

Vivian and Maria were both from a small rural town in Kentucky and had grown up together. Both girls had sweethearts back home and planned to go home every weekend to see them. They already had their lives planned--get a teaching degree, marry their sweethearts, have children, and live happily ever after. Elizabeth told them she was from Louisville and was going to major in art education so that she could teach high school art. She was glad that they would at least have teaching in common.

Her mother and father finally made it back with the clothes rack and dresser. They had to go to three stores to find a clothes rack because the racks were sold out in the first two stores they visited. Her dad joked, "Apparently, I'm not the only father who thought of buying a clothes rack. I guess I'm not as smart as I think I am." Her mother placed the small dresser between the beds and started putting Elizabeth's pajamas and underwear into it. Her father put the clothes rack together and put it in front of the picture window that was in the wall opposite the door. Elizabeth put her own bedspread in a box to be taken home. When he saw the box with the bedspread, her father grumbled, "Not another box to carry back to the car. I'm taking back almost as many boxes as we brought." Before Elizabeth could say anything, he winked at her.

Once everything was unpacked and put away, her parents kissed her goodbye and told her to call them the next weekend or sooner if she needed anything. She thought she saw tears in her father's eyes when he left the room. As soon as they left, she realized that she was on her own for the first time in her life. She climbed up the ladder to her bed and began to get acquainted with Vivian and Maria. Although Elizabeth was still a little overwhelmed, their easy-going manner soon made her feel at ease. *These girls are really nice! I lucked out!*

Elizabeth summed up her life during their conversation. "I'm from Louisville and I went to a small Catholic high school. I'm not dating anyone right now. I had a boyfriend in high school, but he broke up with me on graduation day. We were going to different colleges and he wanted to be free to date other girls. I was hurt at first, but I finally decided that it was for the best because I want to date boys here, too. We weren't really in love anyway. I picked Eastern because it's small and just a couple of hours from home. I'm really glad I ended up with you two. I think we'll have a great time together." She hoped that the three of them would go out and get involved in some of the activities on campus. Sadly, she soon found out that her roommates had no desire to leave the room other than to go to classes or to go to the cafeteria to eat. As luck would have it, most of the girls on her floor were just like Vivian and Maria. They went home every weekend and weren't interested in getting involved in campus life. Elizabeth stayed in with them but it wasn't what she wanted. She wished that she had someone to go out with and have some fun.

She dreaded the weekends because everyone on her floor went home and she was left by herself. She got to know some of the girls who stayed on campus but they were all dating and always with their boyfriends. She hoped that some of the boys in her classes would ask her out, but they bolted out of the classrooms as soon as class was over. When she walked back from her classes, she noticed that the sorority girls all seemed to be having fun. They knew all the guys who hung out on the library steps or in the student center. Sometimes, she noticed that the boys hanging out were looking at her, but she was too shy to stop and talk to them. She soon decided that she needed to be in a sorority if she was ever going to have any fun.

CHAPTER 2

The pads of Elizabeth's fingers drummed on the desk as she willed the second hand on the clock above the teacher's head to move faster. *This is torture!* She still had five more minutes before class was over and she felt like she had been trapped in the class for hours. All she wanted was to get out of the class and return to the dorm. When the bell finally rang, she pushed her way through the door. She ran down the hall, down the stairs, out through the front door, and all the way back to the dorm.

The area in front of the mailboxes overflowed with excited girls. Each time mail slid into a mailbox, the owner of the box scrambled through the crowd to get to it. Elizabeth's box was on the bottom row and she was going to be one of the last girls to get her mail. The wait was maddening. She paced around in the back of the crowd and impatiently waited to see if an envelope would slide into her box. At last, her box was the next one to be filled. She let out the breath she had been holding when an envelope slid into her box.

* * * *

In 1968, Eastern Kentucky University did not allow first semester freshmen to join a fraternity or sorority. The president of the university believed that new students should concentrate on their studies and become accustomed to rigorous, academic demands before joining a social club. He didn't allow sorority or fraternity houses either, but each had its own floor in a dormitory. The second-semester rush policy also gave the sororities and fraternities a chance

13

to check out the freshmen class. By the time rush started at the beginning of the second semester, the sororities and fraternities knew the freshmen with good grades and those who had gotten involved in campus activities.

CHAPTER 3

At the beginning of the second semester, Elizabeth lived by herself because Vivian and Maria had moved to Telford Hall as planned. The girl who was going to be Elizabeth's new roommate had decided not to come back to school at the last minute. By the time she learned that her new roommate wasn't coming back to school, it was too late to find another roommate. She was always by herself and she hated it. Going to rush parties by herself was a stretch for her, but she forced herself to go in the hopes that she would be able to finally start having some fun.

She didn't know any of the sorority girls or many of the freshmen girls who were going out for rush. Despite this fact, she was invited back by several sororities during the last round of rush parties. Being asked to join any one of them would have been okay, but she really wanted to get into what was considered to be the best sorority on campus.

The girls in the best sorority were beautiful, smart, and popular. They were also considered to be the real ladies on the campus. Most of them were fraternity sweethearts, cheerleaders, pompom girls, and/ or campus leaders. They also held the honor of having the highest grade-point average among the sororities. Their floor was located in McGregor Hall, which sat in the middle of campus next to the library and student center.

Elizabeth doubted she would get into that sorority because they were the most popular girls on campus. She had no way of knowing they had decided to pick their pledges from the girls with the highest grades. Making perfect grades her first semester had gotten her to the top of all the sororities' lists. When she was invited back to their last rush party, she held onto a slim hope that she would be asked to join. During that last rush party, the president and pledge trainer spent a great deal of time talking with her. Although she was really nervous, she tried hard to remember to smile while she talked to them. When the president moved on to talk to other girls, the pledge trainer took the time to introduce her to other members. She hoped that this was a good sign.

She saw the envelope slide into her box. *Yes! I got in to the best sorority on campus! I can't believe it!*

CHAPTER 4

After looking through all of her clothes, she picked her favorite kelly-green dress to wear to the new-pledge reception. The bright green color complemented her long brown hair and fit her trim five-foot, six-inch body like a glove. Now that she was in the sorority, she was nervous about fitting in with the beautiful, popular girls. She really didn't know those girls at all and she had no idea who else would be in her pledge class. *What if they don't like me? I'm nothing special. I hope I fit in with them.*

She looked at her reflection in the mirror and realized that she looked scared to death. Silently, she scolded herself for being so nervous. Maria had said that she looked like Natalie Wood but she couldn't see the resemblance. She didn't think she was pretty or ugly, but neither did she consider herself a beauty. Her father always said she was beautiful. However, her mother had told her that she was no prettier than any other girl and being kind to people was more important than looks anyway. Over the years, Elizabeth had come to regard herself as simply ordinary.

As she walked to McGregor Hall to meet her new sorority sisters, Elizabeth thought about Vivian and Maria going home every weekend. *I'd be miserable sitting at home with nothing to do. I love my family but I decided to come here so that I could be on my own. I didn't do anything last semester except sit in the room and study. I certainly didn't come here to stay by myself in a dorm room. I want to be a college girl, not a hermit. Now that I'm in a sorority, maybe I'll have some fun. God, please help me to fit in with those beautiful girls and let them like me.*

CHAPTER 5

When Elizabeth met her new sorority sisters, she realized that she was the only one with brown hair and brown eyes. All of her new sisters were beautiful blondes with blue eyes and they were all smart. The pledge class had a grade-point average of 3.9 out of a possible 4.0. Most of them had been high school homecoming queens and cheerleaders. Once again, she felt like the odd-girl out.

Cathy was assigned to be Elizabeth's big sister in the sorority. Cathy was only five feet tall and had short, curly-blonde hair and blue eyes. She only weighed 85 pounds and she was a real free spirit dynamo. As soon as Elizabeth walked in, Cathy ran over to her and hugged her.

Cathy's words spilled out, "My name is Cathy and I'm your big sister! My job is to take care of you during pledging. My God, you look just like Natalie Wood! I hope you aren't dating anyone special because you are about to become very popular." Elizabeth started to answer but Cathy yelled out, "Look everybody, we have Natalie Wood's double here!" Elizabeth's face turned red as all eyes focused on her. Cathy noticed her embarrassment but ignored it as she started introducing Elizabeth to the other pledges.

Cathy's half of the room was filled with sorority memorabilia and favors from fraternity parties. Her bedspread was covered with discarded clothes. The other side of the room was completely empty except for the bedspread that her roommate left when she moved out to get married over Christmas.

Cathy hated living by herself so she asked Elizabeth to spend the weekend in her room so that they could get know each other better. They got along so well that weekend, that she decided to ask Elizabeth to move in with her.

"We get along really well and I need a roommate. Would you be interested in moving in with me for the rest of the semester? New pledges aren't usually allowed to live on the sorority floor until after initiation, but I can fix that. I know you don't have a roommate and living by yourself really sucks. What do you think? Would you want to be my roommate?"

Elizabeth jumped at the chance, "I would love to live on the sorority floor with you. I think we would be great roommates! Do you really think you can get permission for me to live with you?"

"No problem. I'll make all the arrangements and you can move in next weekend."

Not only did Cathy get permission for Elizabeth to move in with her, she talked three of her fraternity buddies into moving all of Elizabeth's belongings as well. By next Friday afternoon, Elizabeth was happily living with Cathy.

Cathy wanted to go to Hollywood and become a famous actress. From what Elizabeth knew of Cathy, she didn't doubt for an instant that it would happen. The two girls were perfectly suited to be roommates -- Cathy led and Elizabeth followed. Cathy forced Elizabeth to be less reserved and Elizabeth kept Cathy grounded. At least as much as she could ever be grounded. Cathy believed that life was all about taking chances. Why else would she be making plans to move to Hollywood where she didn't know a soul? She had never acted in anything but she believed she would be a star.

CHAPTER 6

Elizabeth thought Cathy must know everyone on campus because everywhere they went, Cathy talked to everyone. Cathy realized right away that Elizabeth wasn't comfortable meeting people on her own and she set out to make sure that Elizabeth became well known on campus. She had Elizabeth meet her in the Student Center every afternoon to introduce her to other students. Also, she took Elizabeth with her everywhere. Cathy never missed anything going on and she made sure that Elizabeth was there for all of it.

If a fraternity guy asked Cathy out, she asked him to get a date for Elizabeth as well. They went to mixers, ballgames, concerts, parties, and formals. Because Cathy believed in living life to its fullest, Elizabeth had more fun that semester than she had experienced in her whole life. As time went by, it became easier for her to stop and chat with the students she met through Cathy. She always made an effort to compliment the girls on their hair or their dress. Also, she listened attentively to what the boys were saying. She soon became one of the most popular girls on campus.

Her sophomore year was a whirlwind. A fraternity known for having wild parties asked her to be their sweetheart because they wanted a sweetheart who was dignified and a real lady. She was pledge trainer for the new pledge class. She served on the inter-dorm counsel and helped to plan charity events for the sorority. She loved every minute of it!

When it came time to vote for the most popular girls on campus, Elizabeth was chosen to represent McGregor Hall. She was flattered to be nominated, but she didn't think she had a chance of winning. Vivian and Maria launched a campaign to get the girls in their dorm to vote for her. With votes from the sorority, the fraternity, McGregor Hall, Vivian and Maria's dorm, and other students she had met, she easily made the top five. When the editor of the yearbook called to tell her that she had won and would be featured in the yearbook as a campus beauty, she was flabbergasted. Cathy thought it was amazing that Elizabeth didn't have a clue how much people loved her or how special she was. Elizabeth still thought of herself as just ordinary.

When she took the yearbook home, her father was as proud as a peacock. Her mother said, although it was nice, Elizabeth had so many pictures in the yearbook, she needed to remember that she was in college to get an education. She could always count on her mother to be practical.

CHAPTER 7

Elizabeth continued to excel in her classes. She loved to paint and liked the idea of helping young students develop their talents. She never thought that her art was particularly good, but her professors were complimentary and encouraging. She always carried a full load of classes and maintained her 4.0 grades with ease until her junior year, when her life changed forever.

Elizabeth's junior year was her last one to have Cathy as a roommate. Cathy would graduate in the spring and she had never wavered from the idea of moving to Hollywood to become a star. Elizabeth had tried to present the practical challenges that Cathy would face in Hollywood, but Cathy dismissed her concerns. Cathy's enthusiasm was infectious and Elizabeth sometimes found herself wishing she could go to Hollywood with her. She wouldn't allow herself to think about what life would be like without Cathy being there for her.

One Wednesday evening, Cathy and Elizabeth went to see the new Clint Eastwood movie, *Play Misty For Me*. Elizabeth was transfixed during the love scene on the bluffs, but she was more interested in the song that was playing in the background than the love scene itself. She had never heard a song that touched her as deeply as *The First Time Ever*. Cathy was ready to bolt from the theater as soon as the movie was over, but Elizabeth grabbed her arm and pulled her back into her seat. She wanted to wait until she saw who sang the song and the song's name before they left. Cathy didn't understand what the big deal was, but Elizabeth explained that she always thought she would fall in love the first time she saw the right guy. The song put her belief into words. Cathy laughed and said love never happened that way in real life.

* * * *

It was 1970 and many of the Vietnam veterans were coming back to the US. They used their GI Bill to get a college education. The rest of the country was in the middle of protesting the war, but Eastern students were, for the most part, not involved in the anti-war movement and the vets easily assimilated into the college.

The vets introduced Eastern students to marijuana. Smoking pot soon became as common as drinking alcohol. The Women's Lib Movement was just beginning and many of the girls on campus began taking birth control pills and stopped wearing bras. The world was changing and Elizabeth wanted to be part of that change. However, she always wore a bra and thought she would remain a virgin until her wedding night.

CHAPTER 8

Thursday night was always party night at Eastern. Because many courses didn't require classes on Friday, students could stay out late on Thursday night and sleep in on Friday mornings. Some, like Vivian and Maria, either went home on Thursday afternoon or prepared to go home on Friday as soon as classes were over. Most students headed downtown to the bars to unwind and line up dates for the weekend. The local police didn't have enough manpower to enforce the age limit on drinking. Unless there was a major disturbance, they usually turned a blind eye on the bars that served students. The bar owners had a behind-the-scenes agreement that they would only sell beer to the students. At twenty-five cents a can, most students never thought to order anything else.

On the Thursday night before homecoming weekend, Elizabeth and three other girls walked into the Bear & Bull, a bar where most of the Greeks hung out. The bar owner had decorated the walls with the emblems of all the fraternities and sororities. His bar was often a major sponsor of charity events they held. That Thursday night, the bar was packed with students getting a jump on celebrating homecoming weekend. As Elizabeth made her way toward a group of her sorority sisters, she was bumped and beer spilled down her blouse. Mortified that she would have a beer stain on her blouse for the rest of the evening, she quickly tried to brush off the beer. She looked up in anger to see who had so clumsily spilled the beer. Her eyes locked onto Gary's eyes and an electric charge ran through her body.

CHAPTER 9

Gary was six-feet tall and muscular. He had a square jaw, jet-black hair, and the most incredible ice-blue eyes she had ever seen. She opened her mouth to speak, But before she could utter a word, Gary yelled above the crowd's noise, "Oh God, I can't believe I just spilled beer on the most beautiful woman I've ever laid eyes on! Please, let me buy you a beer to apologize. My name is Gary". Elizabeth blushed as she stood there thinking she should say something clever but all she could come up with was, "Okay". Gary took her by the arm and led her to a corner at the back of the bar. He told her to wait there while he fought the crowd to get their beers.

She watched Gary as he pushed his way through the crowd. Her face was still warm and her mind reeled with excitement. *Who is that guy and why haven't I seen him before? I would have noticed him. He's gorgeous! Don't be stupid and get your hopes up. He's probably just being nice because he spilled his beer.* She twirled her hair while she waited for him to come back. She wasn't usually nervous when a guy came on to her but he was different. He was older and seemed more mature than the fraternity boys she had dated. She realized she really wanted him to like her. She stopped fiddling with her hair and smiled when he came back with the beers.

* * * *

Gary looked over all the girls as they entered the bar. He had heard that the most beautiful girls on campus hung out at the Bear & Bull. From what he saw, that was true. He had given himself enough time to adjust to taking classes since coming to Eastern that semester and now he wanted to find a girlfriend. *Maybe I'll luck out and find one with a rich daddy.* When Elizabeth walked in, his jaw dropped. She was the most stunning woman he had ever seen--a dead ringer for Natalie Wood. *She is the one I've been looking for! If she's rich, I just hit the jackpot.* He had been making his way to her when someone shoved him and his beer spilled down her blouse. He grabbed the opportunity to meet her.

*　*　*　*

When Gary finally made it back with their beers, he stood close to Elizabeth. He leaned in and tried to make sure she could hear him above the loud chatter going on around them. Ordinarily, she didn't like having someone invade her personal space, but she didn't mind Gary being close.

He began the conversation by saying he had just gotten out of the Army and he had served in Vietnam. He had an apartment off campus and was majoring in business. *No wonder I've never seen him before. He's new and lives off campus.* Gary told her it was surreal being in college after the things he had seen and done while in the service. He didn't say what things he had seen or done, and she didn't ask. She had heard that the vets were closed mouth about what they had been through in Nam. Everyone that knew those poor boys had endured unimaginable horrible things over there.

Elizabeth found herself telling him about her love of art and aspirations of one day being able to sell some of her work. She had never opened up like this to any guy in the past. Gary was easy to talk to and he seemed interested in everything she had to say. He told her, "I was a wild kid in high school and didn't want to go to college. My number came up in the draft and I grew up real fast. When I got out of the Army, I decided to get an education on Uncle Sam's dime."

When they finished their beers, Gary asked if he could walk her to the dorm. She eagerly agreed because she wanted to get to know him, and it was almost impossible to carry on a conversation in the bar. Gary put his arm around her as they slowly walked to the dorm. Having his arm around her made her feel safe and protected. Gary suggested they sit on the top row of the amphitheater at the center of campus to continue their conversation because the dorm lobby would be crowded. He held her hand as they talked. His touch made her feel warm and tingly. He asked about her family and about her father's occupation. She thought he was genuinely interested in the details of her life. By the time they stood up to continue their walk to the dorm, everyone knew she was already falling hard for him.

As Gary had predicted, the dorm lobby was crowded with girls saying, "Goodnight," to their dates. With his arm still around her shoulder, he guided her to the side of the lobby.

He said, "I know this is short notice and I'll understand if you say 'No,' but please have dinner with me tomorrow night."

She smiled and quickly answered, "Well, of course. What time?"

"I'll pick you up at six. Wear a pretty dress." She was shocked when he dramatically took her hand and lifted it to his lips. He kept his eyes locked on hers as he kissed her hand. Without saying another word, he turned and left the dorm. She stood frozen to the floor-- completely dazzled.

Gary smiled to himself as he walked back downtown. He had been looking for a woman who was not only beautiful but intelligent, as well. Elizabeth had everything he wanted in a woman except that she didn't have a rich daddy. In spite of that, he wasn't going to let this opportunity go to waste. He would make sure she was his by the end of the weekend.

CHAPTER 10

Cathy got back to the dorm room a few hours later. When she walked into the room, she knew immediately that something was different about Elizabeth. "What's up? You look different! You're positively glowing!" Elizabeth laughed and said, "I am glowing. I think I'm in love! It happened just like in the movies! I met a guy who's new here. When I looked at him, I felt like I was hit by lightning." Cathy jumped onto Elizabeth's bed and laughed, "What?! Tell me! Who is this wonderful man? Do I know him? Where did you meet him? What does he look like? Details, I need details!" Cathy always spoke quickly when she was excited. Elizabeth picked up the stuffed bear Cathy had given her and hugged it protectively to her chest as she told Cathy all about Gary.

"He's gorgeous. He's six-feet tall with black hair, and he has the most incredible blue eyes I've ever seen. He's a vet and he just started here this semester. I felt all tingly when he touched me. I really think that I'm already in love with him." Cathy giggled and clapped her hands through the whole story. "Love at first sight! I never believed it actually ever happened until now. Wow!" As long as Cathy had known her, Elizabeth had never shown the least bit of interest in having a relationship with any guy she dated. There had been plenty of guys who wanted a relationship with her, but she had always moved on to the next date and waited for 'Mr. Right' to come along. Cathy couldn't wait to meet him. She knew he had to be something else.

When Elizabeth's alarm went off at seven the next morning, she did something she'd never done before. She turned off the alarm and skipped the one class she had that day. She spent the day going through her wardrobe, searching for the right dress to wear for Gary. Cathy watched in amazement as Elizabeth fretted over each dress. Cathy had never seen her so concerned about what to wear. A pile of discarded dresses grew on the floor next to Elizabeth's closet.

Around noon, it dawned on Cathy that Elizabeth already had a date for the weekend. "What are you going to do about your homecoming date? He's the president of the fraternity and you can't just leave him without a date!" Elizabeth's homecoming date included a Friday night reception for the fraternity's alumni, the football game Saturday afternoon, and a formal party on Saturday night. Elizabeth dropped the black dress she had in her hands.

"Oh, God, I forgot! You've got to get me out of it. Call him and say that I have an emergency and can't make it. Please find him another date. You've got to help me! I wouldn't do this if Gary was just another guy, but he isn't. Please do something."

"Okay, okay, no problem. I'll take care of it. I've never seen you so excited about a guy and there's no way I'll let you miss this date. Just give me a minute to think of something." Cathy smiled as she said, "I know! Karen just broke up with Jerry and she needs a date. I'll fix her up with your date." Cathy left to find Karen. Elizabeth was surprised that she was willing to lie to get out of a date when she had just met Gary. She had never done anything like that before and she felt guilty. *Please, God, forgive me for lying.*

Cathy was all smiles when she walked back into the room and announced that everything was arranged. Karen was grateful to be able to go to the homecoming festivities with a date that would make Jerry jealous. Elizabeth's date was considered a big man on campus and Karen couldn't believe Elizabeth was dumping him, but she was thrilled she wouldn't miss homecoming. Cathy laughed, "Everybody is happy and life is great!" *Cathy always comes through for me. What am I going to do without her?*

Gary arrived at the dorm promptly at six that evening. Because men weren't allowed beyond the reception desk, he called her room from the lobby to let her know he had arrived. She let the phone ring twice before answering. Cathy had drummed it into her to not appear too eager. She took one last look at herself in the mirror. The kelly-green dress still fit her like a glove. She began to panic that maybe he wouldn't think she was so great after all. *Why am I so nervous? He's just another date. No, that's not true. I've been waiting for him all my life.* She took a calming breath and let it out slowly before she left the room. By the time the elevator arrived at the lobby, she appeared to be calm, although her stomach was turning flip flops. Gary walked through the crowded lobby and grabbed both of her hands. He held her at arms' length and looked her up and down. He exclaimed, "I didn't dream it! I have a date with the most beautiful woman in the world!" Everyone in the lobby stared at the scene he created. She blushed and lowered her head to avoid the eyes trained on her. Gary put his arm around her shoulder as they walked out of the lobby. They were a beautiful couple.

CHAPTER 11

Gary took her to a restaurant next to the Kentucky River where college students and townspeople gathered to eat beer cheese, steaks, and drink pitchers of ice-cold beer. The restaurant was filled to capacity because it was homecoming weekend. She thought it was amazing when they were seated within minutes of arriving at the restaurant. The romantic table for two was nestled in the back corner of the dimly-lit dining room. A red hurricane candle cast a flickering light on the red-and-white, checkered tablecloth. Gary laughed when she commented on how fast they were seated. He admitted he had come to the restaurant earlier and slipped the hostess $20 to keep the table free for them. She was impressed! Twenty dollars was a big sum of money.

Gary ordered a pitcher of beer and the best steaks on the menu. She barely touched her beer and only took small bites of her steak as she listened intently to everything Gary said.

He smiled easily as he shared memories of his travels. "I went to Australia on R & R. The night sky was beautiful there. I went to the beach every night and sat for hours just looking at the stars. They seemed so close I felt like I could reach out and touch them. I really want to go back there someday. Maybe we'll go together." He was sweeping her off her feet and stealing her heart with every word he spoke.

CHAPTER 12

After dinner, Gary asked if she would go with him to his apartment for a nightcap and she quickly agreed. When they arrived at the apartment, she was impressed again. It was clean and tastefully furnished. Most apartments of the boys she had dated were decorated with posters of Raquel Welch and coffee tables made from industrial wire spools. He had framed prints on the walls and comfortable furniture. Mementos he had collected while in the service decorated the tables and bookshelf. He suggested she put on some music while he went into the kitchen to get their drinks. She looked through his record collection and picked a Johnny Mathis album. *Misty* was playing when he came back into the living room with their drinks.

Gary brought in two glasses of white wine and remarked, "I noticed that you're not much of a beer drinker. I bought some wine thinking that you might like it." Elizabeth accepted the wine glass and tentatively took a sip. She had never tasted wine before and she liked the clean, crisp taste. *How sophisticated!* They talked about art, music, and the classes they were taking. He seemed genuinely interested in her opinions. While they talked, she kicked off her shoes and curled up on the couch next to him. She was completely at ease with him.

Gary was in the middle of a sentence when he stopped talking. He leaned in and gently kissed Elizabeth on her lips. A thrill rushed through her and she knew that she would remember that moment for the rest of her life. He pulled her close as he kissed her again. This time, his mouth seemed to devour her lips as his tongue flickered in and out of her mouth. His hands caressed her back and breasts. She responded to his kisses and wanted more, but she pulled away when his hand slid between her legs. He kept kissing her and, the next time his hand touched her thigh, she didn't pull away. He stood up and pulled her to her feet. Without saying a word, he scooped her up and carried her to his bedroom. She trembled as he unzipped her dress. She had never been this far with a man before. Elizabeth stammered, "Wait, I-I-I've never made love before. I'm not sure…"

Gary murmured, "It's okay. I love you. I fell in love with you as soon as I saw you. I'll be gentle."

He deeply kissed her as he lowered her to his bed. Although she had always thought she would be a virgin on her wedding night, she gave herself completely to Gary. She was already deeply in love with him and believed he felt the same.

Gary was a considerate and passionate lover. He made love slowly and tenderly. He made sure that she was taken to heights of pleasure she had never known. She willingly gave herself completely as he explored her body. Her fear dissipated as her body responded when they became one. He held her in his arms long after they finished making love. She snuggled, as closely as possible, and nuzzled her head on his chest. She had never been happier. *He truly loves me!*

After they snuggled for a while, Gary said, "I'll draw you a warm bath so that you can soak for a while. I know you must be sore and it'll help." *He is so sweet and knows just what to do.*

As he left the room to start the bath water, she lay her head back on the pillow and happily thought, *He loves me and we're going to get married!* Naked, she walked unashamed into the bathroom and stepped into the tub. Gary climbed into the tub and pulled her down to his end of the tub. He arranged her so that her back was resting on his chest with his muscular arms wrapped around her. He held her tight until the water began to cool, then helped her out of the tub. Gary used a towel to dry off and he gently patted her dry. He picked her up and carried her back to his bed. This time, however, he curled up next to her and quickly fell asleep. She smiled as she listened to his steady breathing. She had never been so happy nor felt so loved. She stayed at his apartment the entire weekend.

CHAPTER 13

Elizabeth returned to the dorm on Sunday evening just as the sun was setting. When she walked into the room, Cathy jumped off her bed and hugged her. "Man, when you go, you go all the way!"

Elizabeth blushed and smiled. She said she was indeed in love and had 'been with' the man of her dreams. She was too modest to give intimate details, but Cathy knew Elizabeth had given herself completely to Gary and was totally in love.

Cathy laughed as she said, "First thing tomorrow, we get you on the pill." Elizabeth blushed again but agreed that would be a good idea.

Donna, a sorority sister who lived across the hall, came in to talk about homecoming weekend. Elizabeth thought of Donna as a real-life Barbie doll. Donna had long, blonde hair, blue eyes, and a perfect hourglass figure. She had a dry sense of humor that always made Elizabeth laugh. Donna was also dating a veteran whom she considered to be the man of her dreams. The three girls talked for hours.

Cathy announced, "I met a pharmacist at the drug store and he's really cute. I'm going to go out with him next weekend. I'm tired of dating college boys."

Donna nodded, "Older men are definitely the way to go. They seem to know how to do everything. More worldly... I guess. They make college boys seem so immature."

Elizabeth blushed as she said, "They definitely know how to make a woman feel special. When I'm with Gary, I feel so secure and loved. I can't imagine my life without him. Everything happened so quickly but I'm really in love with him. I know we'll get married someday. He told me that he loves me. In fact, he said he fell in love with me the minute he saw me."

Cathy laughed, "I suspect Gary is great in bed and that doesn't hurt either." Elizabeth threw the stuffed bear at Cathy, but she was grinning from ear to ear.

When Elizabeth came back from class the next day, she was surprised to find a vase of her sorority's flowers for her at the receptionist's desk. Girls who were returning from class gathered around Elizabeth as she opened the card. The flowers were from Gary and he had written the card himself. "These flowers pale in comparison to your beauty! All my love forever. Gary." *He's so sweet he even took the time to find out what flower is the sorority flower. He thinks of everything.*

* * * *

Gary was surprised when he realized that she was still a virgin. He knew that he had to tell her he loved her to get her into his bed. At that point, he would have said and done anything to possess her. Over the weekend, he taught her how to pleasure a man and she was a willing student. He had planned to marry his hometown girlfriend Tanya, but she had broken up with him to become engaged to a rich guy she met at college. Tanya's engagement wrecked his plans to get his hands on her father's fortune. Elizabeth was beautiful and smart, but not rich. He really wanted a rich wife. Until he found a rich girl, he knew he would enjoy the ride.

CHAPTER 14

As Elizabeth and Gary continued to date during that semester, Gary grew more and more demanding of her time. He wanted her to be with him whenever she wasn't in class. He told her how to dress and how to wear her hair. He continued to order her food without asking her what she wanted. Although Elizabeth was mildly irritated with his behavior at times, she never let it show. She told herself he was no different now than when she first met him. She wanted to please him and did anything he asked.

Gary made it clear that he didn't want her to talk to other men. At a sorority party, he created a scene when another guy asked her to dance. When they left the party, she tried to tell him that the guy was just a friend. Gary barked, "No guy is just a friend. All they want to do is get into your pants. You were flirting with him. I saw you. I won't stand for it."

She objected, "I wasn't flirting… I was just talking to him. Please don't be mad at me. I didn't do anything."

"We wouldn't be having this argument if you hadn't been flirting. It's your fault. I won't be with a woman that I can't trust. You really embarrassed me. Don't try to make excuses for yourself. You know what you did."

She was devastated by his comments and was afraid to provoke him any further. She appeased him, "I'm sorry. You're right. He probably did think I was flirting. I won't do it again. Don't be mad anymore. Please!"

"Okay, but you need to watch yourself. I'll walk away and never look back if I can't trust you." The thought that he could just walk away sent a chill through her. *Surely, he doesn't mean that he could walk away so easily. I'd just die if he left me!* After that night, she made sure to stay by Gary's side and let him do all the talking when they were around other guys. If he left her side when men were around, she went to the ladies' room. The only time she was totally at ease was when they were alone.

Cathy constantly told Elizabeth that Gary was a control freak and she should stand up for herself. She always defended Gary when Cathy said anything about his jealousy. She couldn't bring herself to tell Cathy that he had threatened to walk away, and she was afraid that he would do it if she wasn't careful. Cathy would just say, "Good riddance."

Elizabeth actually thought that if she went along with his demands, things would get better when they were married. There was no doubt in her mind that they would get married because she thought he loved her as much as she loved him. She began to drop hints about wanting to get married when she graduated. Gary ignored her hints but made it appear as if he was thinking about it. He had become a master at getting what he wanted from her without really giving anything back. Sending a few flowers here and there was all it took. By the end of the semester, she was happily cooking his meals, cleaning his apartment, ironing his shirts, and sleeping with him anytime he wanted.

On Wednesday, during the final exam week, Elizabeth talked to her male lab partner after their final. She saw Gary walk toward them and instantly knew that he was furious. In order to avoid a scene, she quickly said "Goodbye" to her lab partner and walked over to Gary. He grabbed her by the arm and practically dragged her away. Once they got to a place where they were alone, Gary screamed, "Who the hell was he? Were you seeing him behind my back?"

She tried to explain, "He's my lab partner, and we were talking about the project we turned in."

Gary screamed, "You're lying!"

Tears spilled down her cheeks but they only seemed to fuel his anger. Gary screamed, "Don't try to use fake tears on me. It won't work! I thought you were different from other women, but you're not. You can't be trusted!" He turned and stomped away.

"Gary, wait!" She tried to catch up to him but he had started to run. She made it back to her dorm room before she completely fell apart.

Cathy came back from taking a final exam to find Elizabeth lying on her bed and crying. "Now what?"

"Gary went crazy! He says that I can't be trusted, but I can. I was just talking to my lab partner. I would never cheat on Gary. I love him."

Cathy tried to reassure her, "He has been a jealous asshole lately, but he's probably just stressed out about finals. He'll get over it."

"He is jealous but this time was different. I've never seen him like that. His face was red and he yelled at me. I didn't do anything wrong! I need to talk to him to straighten this out before I go home. I can't lose him over this. I just can't!" She tried to call him to talk it out but he didn't answer his phone. Cathy knew there was nothing she could say that would help, so she went to visit Donna while Elizabeth continued to call Gary's apartment.

Elizabeth's exams were finished that day and she had planned to go home for semester break that evening. When Gary didn't answer the phone, she called her parents to tell them she wouldn't be home until Friday. They were disappointed that they would have to wait to see her, but told her to drive safely on the way home. During the next two days, Elizabeth called Gary's apartment repeatedly. He didn't answer. He had left town right after his encounter with Elizabeth.

* * * *

On Wednesday before finals were over, Gary's father had called with news that Tanya was home from college and announced that she had broken her engagement. Gary knew he would see her while he was home.

After his father's call, Gary weighed his options. *Elizabeth is beautiful and Tanya is just so-so. Elizabeth is very intelligent and Tanya is smart but lacks common sense. Elizabeth is really built and Tanya is skinny. I can easily control both girls. Elizabeth lacks one thing that Tanya has--money. Ballgame over!* He knew he would do whatever it took to get Tanya back and he wasn't going to blow it this time.

When he saw Elizabeth talking to that guy, he knew it was a perfect opportunity to be free to pursue 'his Tanya' again. Until that moment, he had planned to see Tanya without breaking up with Elizabeth first. This way was much better. He could truthfully tell Tanya that he wasn't dating anyone. If things didn't work out with Tanya, he could easily get Elizabeth back when school started after the break. As soon as he arrived at his parents' house, he called Tanya and asked her for a date.

CHAPTER 15

While Elizabeth was home over the break, her father noticed that she was anxious most of the time. "What's going on? I can tell you're upset. Did something happen with that guy you've been dating?" Elizabeth denied anything was wrong. She was worried that if her family knew that Gary had dumped her, it would be a topic of conversation during the entire break. She couldn't deal with their questions and it was safer to keep her family in the dark. Luckily, he didn't press any further after he asked a few questions and got no answers. Elizabeth hoped he would call to wish her Merry Christmas or Happy New Year and they could get things straightened out. He didn't call.

Her parents went 'all out' for Christmas that year because they missed having her at home. Elizabeth spent hours baking cookies and making fudge to take to church to share after the Christmas Day service. Her father decorated the Christmas tree and hung the outdoor lights while the Elizabeth and her mother baked. Her mother cooked their favorite dishes for Christmas Eve dinner. When everyone got up on Christmas morning, beautifully-wrapped presents had magically appeared under the tree. Her father laughed and said that everyone must have been really good that year because Santa had gone overboard with the presents.

Although Elizabeth enjoyed being home with her family, she couldn't stop thinking about Gary. During the Christmas Day church service, Elizabeth said a silent prayer. *Dear God, thank you for giving me Gary. I love him so much. Help me to be the woman he wants me to be. Please let him know that I would never cheat on him. Thank you for giving me such a wonderful Christmas with my family. Help me be a better person and forgive my sins. In Jesus' name, I pray. Amen.*

When Elizabeth returned to Eastern after the break, she still hoped that Gary had gotten over his jealousy. They could go back to the way they had been when they first started dating. He hadn't called her during the break, but she convinced herself that he must have lost her parents' phone number. Although she knew Cathy wouldn't approve, she called Gary's apartment as soon as she entered her dorm room.

Gary hadn't given Elizabeth much thought while he spent every possible moment with Tanya. Elizabeth had been a nice diversion, but now he was fully focused on winning the grand prize. He knew he would have to break up with her as soon as he got back to Eastern. If he saw her again, he might want to sleep with her and that would not be good for anyone. He had given Tanya a heart-shaped diamond necklace for Christmas and she was already dropping hints about getting engaged on Valentine's Day. His phone rang as he unlocked his apartment door and he knew it had to be Elizabeth. He already knew what he was going to say to her.

"Hello."

Elizabeth said, "Gary, I . . ."

Before she could get out another word, Gary said, "Elizabeth, I want to apologize for the way I acted last time I saw you. The stress of final exams got to me and I took it out on you. I thought about us over the break and I do care about you. You're incredible. However, I realized that I'm just not ready for a serious relationship right now. It would be unfair to you to keep dating. I'm sorry."

He hung up the phone without allowing her to say a word. She was stunned. She never dreamed that he could be so cold and uncaring. She was still holding the phone when her legs buckled and she slid down the wall to the floor. She looked at the picture of Gary, which was on her desk, and began to sob. She had given herself completely to him and he had thrown her away as easily as an empty beer can. *I did everything I could to please him. I thought we were going to get married! How could he do this to me!? I love him with all my heart! My life is ruined!*

CHAPTER 16

About an hour later, the dorm room door flew open. Cathy backed in as she dragged her heavy suitcase and yelled that she was back. She stopped in her tracks when she saw Elizabeth on the floor crying. Elizabeth hadn't moved and was still holding the phone in her hand. Cathy took the receiver from her hand and put it back on the hook. "What the hell happened now?" she asked as she pulled Elizabeth from the floor and sat her on her bed.

"Gary dumped me! He said he wasn't ready for a serious relationship. How could he have done that? He knows that I love him with all my heart! I gave myself completely to him and I thought he loved me. I thought we were going to get married. I didn't mean anything to him or else he wouldn't have been so cruel. Why would he use me and throw me away like that? I can't ever show my face in public again! I was such a fool to believe that it really was love at first sight for both of us. My life is ruined!"

Cathy said, "Gary's an asshole and a control freak. He doesn't deserve you." Her words sent Elizabeth into another sobbing fit. She retracted her words but it didn't help. Elizabeth couldn't be comforted by anything she said. The longer Elizabeth sobbed the more concerned Cathy became.

Elizabeth's eyes were red and her eyelids began to swell from crying for so long. Her whole body trembled as she rocked back and forth on her bed. Cathy ran cold water on a washcloth. "Lie down and put this on your eyes. I'll be back in about half an hour."

Elizabeth did as she was told, but she kept mumbling that her life was over. Lying down caused her tears to run down the side of her face and into her hair. She was a mess and she didn't care. She truly believed her life was ruined forever.

Cathy went to the pharmacist she was dating for help. "My roommate's hysterical! She's been crying for hours. The guy she was dating dumped her. Because she slept with him, she thinks her life is over. I can't get her to calm down and I've tried everything I can think of. Can you give me something to help her?"

"I'll call a doctor I play golf with. He can authorize a script for a few Valium. They'll help get her calmed down."

"That would be great because she really needs help. I wouldn't ask you to do this but I'm at my wit's end. I've never seen anyone so upset unless they knew someone had died." He smiled at her exaggeration while he was dialing the phone.

When he hung up with the doctor, he said, "He gave me a script for ten Valium. If she needs more, she'll have to see him. This should be enough to get her through a few days. By that time, maybe you can talk some sense into her. Her life isn't ruined just because she slept with some guy."

"You're the most wonderful man in the world! Thank you for helping us. I promise I'll make it up to you." Cathy winked at him and took the pills back to the dorm.

When she got back to the room, Elizabeth hadn't moved. Her tears had finally stopped, but she just lay there, staring at the ceiling. "Snap out of it. You're a complete basket case!" Cathy's words started Elizabeth's tears again.

Cathy waited until the latest round of crying ended and pulled the prescription bottle out of her purse. She filled a glass with water and handed it to Elizabeth, along with the bottle of pills.

"Take one. It'll help you relax."

"What is it?" Elizabeth asked as she opened the bottle.

"Valium. In the history of the world, nobody has ever needed a Valium more than you do. Now take one. You'll feel better."

Elizabeth swallowed one of the Valium and curled into a fetal position. After a while, she fell into a deep sleep and slept for a few hours. She did feel a little calmer when she woke up, but she was still very upset. She tried to call Gary again but he didn't answer. Cathy told her not to call him because he wasn't going to answer the phone. Elizabeth knew that was true and stopped calling him. She continued to take the Valium for the next three days, but she didn't go to her classes. When she wasn't asleep, she paced back and forth in the small room. Their window overlooked the quad and she constantly looked out the window in the hopes that she would see Gary. Cathy told her to stop it because the only reason Gary would be in the quad was if he was coming to see her, and that wasn't going to happen. The one time she left the room was when she went to the registrar's office and dropped all of her classes, except the one art class she was taking. She was afraid that the other classes might be in the same buildings as Gary's classes.

By the middle of the week, Cathy was truly worried about her. She wasn't snapping out of it and she drove Cathy nuts with the constant pacing and crying. Hoping that two heads would be better than one, Cathy told Donna about Elizabeth's emotional condition. Donna took a bag of Oreos to Elizabeth and tried to tell her that everything would be okay. She tried to convince Elizabeth that her life wasn't ruined because of Gary. "You had sex and it's no big deal. If a guy really loves you, anything you did in the past won't matter. Look at you! You're beautiful, smart, and talented! I have no idea why Gary did what he did, but I do know that he lost the best thing he could ever have. He was lucky to have had you in his life and he blew it. At some point in his life, he'll realize what he lost. The best thing you can do now is to move on and forget about him."

"I appreciate what you are telling me, but don't you see that it's not just about losing my virginity? I've lost my ability to ever trust a man again! He said he loved me, but he just said that to get me into bed. He used me and threw me away when he was done. I can't forgive him and I can't forgive myself for being so stupid."

"You weren't stupid. You were in love for the first time in your life and he took advantage of that." Tears filled Elizabeth's eyes again.

Donna knew that nothing else she could say would make a difference because losing the ability to trust was as bad as it gets. "Eat your cookies and try to feel better." She hugged Elizabeth and left her to eat the cookies.

Once the Valium ran out, Elizabeth didn't sleep much and she only ate food from the vending machine. Cathy tried to talk her into seeing the doctor to get more pills, but she refused because she was too humiliated to tell him about what Gary had done. Cathy was at the end of her rope dealing with her. "Get a grip and move on. You can't keep living like this." Elizabeth didn't respond, but she went over and looked out of the window again. Cathy knew she had to come up with something to help her.

She finally came up with a plan to get Elizabeth to at least leave the room and start living again. "I have a friend, Trisha, who has some pot and she's willing to share. Let's go and see her."

"Pot is illegal! Besides, I don't know Trisha and I don't feel like going out."

"You don't have to smoke the pot if you don't want to, but a change of scenery will do you good. Maybe the pot will help you chill out. Anyway, everybody smokes pot these days."

After putting up several more useless arguments, Elizabeth finally agreed to go to Trisha's. The dorm room had begun to feel like a prison, but she was afraid that she would run into Gary if she went out. Trisha's apartment was on the opposite side of town from Gary's so there was little chance she would see him there. She had never smoked pot but her friends said it made them feel mellow. She decided it was worth a try. Anything would be better than the way she was feeling now.

CHAPTER 17

Trisha was a free spirit like Cathy. Her apartment was decorated in the style of a true flower child. She had black lights, psychedelic posters, and a waterbed. There were big pillows on the floor. The apartment smelled of vanilla from the candles burning on a bookshelf made from old boards and bricks. A James Taylor album was playing on her stereo when Cathy and Elizabeth arrived. They sat on the pillows on the floor. Elizabeth instantly liked Trisha because she was even more uninhibited than Cathy.

Once everyone was settled, Trisha lit a joint and passed the joint to Cathy. Cathy took a hit and passed the joint to Elizabeth, but Elizabeth didn't take it. She admitted that she had never smoked pot and didn't know how. Trisha took the joint back and dramatically demonstrated how to hold the joint, suck in the smoke, and hold the smoke in her lungs. She acted as if she were teaching first graders by using big hand gestures and small words. Cathy laughed at Trisha's demonstration. Elizabeth smiled but she didn't laugh. Trisha handed the joint back to Elizabeth and told her to give it a try. She took a small hit and passed it over to Cathy. They passed the joint back and forth as they sat for a while without talking. Trisha went into the kitchen and came back with a bottle of wine and three glasses. She poured the wine and proposed a toast to happiness. They clicked their glasses together and took a drink. Elizabeth finally relaxed after a few more hits on the joint and had finished a glass of wine. Soon, the three girls were really enjoying themselves. They talked about everything from school to men.

Elizabeth finally opened up and recounted everything that had happened with Gary. Trisha agreed with Cathy that he must be an idiot to let someone as wonderful as Elizabeth go. When the song *You've Got A Friend* began to play, Trisha sang along loudly and pointed to Elizabeth and to herself. They howled with laughter. It was the first time Elizabeth laughed since before the split with Gary in December, and it felt good to laugh again. Elizabeth dramatically declared, "I love pot!" and they laughed hysterically. They were stoned.

Chapter 18

That spring semester, Elizabeth threw herself into helping to organize charity events for the sorority, and she worked on the student committee to plan the dedication of the Meditation Chapel. She often visited Trisha but she refused to go on any dates and never went to the bars on Thursday nights. Cathy knew that the real reason why Elizabeth wouldn't go out was because she was afraid she might see Gary and wouldn't be able handle it. Cathy finally gave up trying to get her to go out.

Cathy broke up with the pharmacist because he wanted to get married and settle down. She definitely did not want to get married. She finalized her plans to move to Hollywood when the semester was over. Elizabeth and Trisha decided that they would rent a two-bedroom apartment for the coming year. Elizabeth didn't want to stay in the dorm if Cathy wasn't going to be there with her.

Elizabeth changed her home address on file with the university to Trisha's apartment because she didn't want her parents to know she had only taken one class that semester. They wouldn't understand why being dumped by Gary would make her not want to go to classes, and she would have to explain everything endlessly. There was no way she would ever let her parents know she had lost her virginity to a guy who had just used her and thrown her away. It would kill them.

When the semester ended, Cathy tearfully said goodbye to Elizabeth and promised to stay in touch. After only one day at home with her parents, she left for Hollywood to become a movie star. As soon as she arrived in Hollywood, she took a job as a waitress and enrolled in an acting class. During the second week she was in Hollywood, she met an actor who starred in a TV detective show. They moved in together within weeks of meeting. Needless to say, she didn't stay in touch with Elizabeth.

CHAPTER 19

Elizabeth went home for the summer and worked in a clothing store. She saved the money she made because she had plans to share an apartment with Trisha. They didn't have a problem with her living off campus. She was over 21 and could make her own decisions. With Elizabeth using the money she made from her summer job to pay the rent, it wasn't going to cost them anything more than if she lived in the dorm.

When Elizabeth's parents finally remembered to ask about her grades, she told them that the grades must have been lost in the mail. They accepted the explanation without question. She always had perfect grades before and there was no reason to think that the last semester had been any different. Elizabeth truthfully told them that her grades were perfect because she made an A in the art class.

The fall of her senior year, Elizabeth moved into the apartment with Trisha and she was totally free for the first time in her life. The dorms on campus had curfews and rules. The only rule in their new apartment was "No Rules Allowed." She took a full load of classes that year and did well in them. Trisha picked up where Cathy left off and tried to get Elizabeth to believe in herself again, but Elizabeth was still not able to take that first step and go out on a date. Trisha was able to see the big picture in life and believed that everything would be fine if Elizabeth relaxed and enjoyed each day. Elizabeth thought God had brought Trisha into her life specifically to help her and she thanked him every day for his intervention. She was beginning to believe in herself a little bit again.

Donna's boyfriend lived a few doors down from their apartment. Although she officially lived in the dorm, Donna practically lived with her boyfriend and she frequently visited Elizabeth and Trisha. Elizabeth wished she had someone special in her life like Donna had, but she still distrusted men and wondered if she would ever trust a man again.

Donna completely understood Elizabeth's reluctance to start dating again, but that didn't stop her from making sure Elizabeth went to all the informal parties held at the apartment complex. Donna told her boyfriend what Gary had done to Elizabeth and how emotionally fragile she was. He had met Gary at a Veteran's Club meeting and thought he was a pompous jerk. He quietly spread the word to guys living in the complex to treat Elizabeth like a sister. All the guys liked Elizabeth and went the extra mile to make her feel comfortable. None of them tried to put the moves on her. As a result, the wall she had built to protect herself gradually came down.

CHAPTER 20

Donna dropped by Elizabeth's apartment one Saturday afternoon about a month before the spring semester ended. Elizabeth was worried, "I have to go to summer school because I still need two classes to graduate. Trisha is graduating and our lease is up at the end of the semester. I really can't afford an apartment by myself but I won't live in the dorm again."

Donna laughed, "I dropped a couple of classes last year and I need two more classes to graduate, too. I really don't want to come back next year. I checked, and the classes I need are being offered this summer. We could get an apartment together with a summer lease and we would have a great time."

"I'd like to have a bigger place. Let's check out the townhouses across the street. They don't cost any more than this apartment and we wouldn't feel like we were right on top of each other."

"Okay, I think they're furnished so we wouldn't have to buy furniture, and we could have a grill on the patio." They rented a townhouse that day and didn't even need to pay a deposit.

Their townhouse had an eat-in kitchen, a living room downstairs, and two bedrooms and a bathroom upstairs. All the apartments and townhouses were filled with students going to summer school, and there was always a party going on somewhere that summer.

Donna worked a part-time job, took classes, and continued to date her boyfriend. Elizabeth finally started to casually date again, and she often hiked in the woods with a guy who lived a couple of doors from their townhouse. Being in the woods relaxed her. Donna thought that Elizabeth becoming a nature lover was hysterical, but she was glad that Elizabeth was having fun.

Because of the small graduating class, their graduation ceremony was held at the amphitheater instead of in the gymnasium. When Elizabeth walked across the stage to receive her diploma, she thought back to the night when she and Gary sat on the top row of the amphitheater. It seemed like a lifetime had passed since that night. She wondered if he knew how much he had hurt her or if he even cared. As she left the stage, she promised herself she would never let a man destroy her self-esteem again.

Donna and Elizabeth threw a big party after the ceremony was over. The living room, kitchen, front porch, and patio were filled with celebrating students. A guy with a cast on his foot was asleep on the couch and they painted his toenails hot pink while he was sleeping. At midnight, they sang *Auld Lang Syne* and drank champagne to welcome their new lives. By all accounts, it was the best party of the summer.

The morning after the party, Donna and Elizabeth took a break from loading their cars and cleaning the mess from the party. They sat at the kitchen table drinking Tab when Elizabeth said, "I wish the summer wasn't ending. I'm a little scared of what's going to happen next. I've tried to picture my life from here but I just draw a blank."

Donna agreed, "I feel the same way. All the girls I know are going to be teachers. I majored in marketing and I have no clue where I'm going to find a job."

Elizabeth said, "So many of our friends are getting married and they have their lives planned out. I don't even have a job lined up yet. I'm not ready to be a teacher now because I would love to be able to travel and learn more about painting. I may even get married someday but, right now, I just feel lost."

"As crazy as college was, at least we knew what to expect. I guess being afraid of the future is natural. We'll just have to handle what life throws at us. Let's finish loading the cars and go to lunch before we drive off into the great unknown."

Elizabeth laughed at that, "Unknown is right. I guess the best I can hope for is that I don't end up living out of my car."

The thought of Elizabeth living in a Volkswagen Bug cracked up Donna. She was still laughing when she picked up a box and headed out to her car. Elizabeth didn't move from the table. *I wish I could stay here, in this time, forever, where it's safe and I know what to expect.*

Please, God, give me the strength to face what lies ahead.

LIFE

CHAPTER 21

Elizabeth moved into a cheap apartment as soon as she returned to Louisville and started looking for a job. Her parents gave her some furniture that they weren't using and paid her first month's rent. They brought dishes, pots, pans, and extra linens for her to use until she was able to buy what she wanted. Elizabeth was set to start her new life if she could just find a job.

Donna moved to Lexington where she was hired as a sales representative for a pharmaceutical company. She rented an apartment in an upscale complex which was filled with young singles who were recent college graduates with new jobs. Her new apartment had a spiral staircase and a fireplace in the upstairs' bedroom. The bedroom also had a small balcony which overlooked a beautiful, wooded area. She thought it was the greatest apartment she could ever have.

Donna and her boyfriend parted ways soon after she moved to Lexington. He had never talked about marriage and she decided that it was time to move on. She knew there was no point in continuing to date if he didn't love her enough to make a long-term commitment. She met new men and went out on many dates.

The first time Elizabeth came to visit, she stood on the spiral staircase and pretended to be Doris Day singing *Ce Sera Sera*. Donna made the comment that Elizabeth could sing professionally, if she wanted. On Sunday afternoon that weekend, someone who lived in Donna's building ran an extension cord to the middle of the parking lot and took a TV out there so that everyone in the building could watch a football game together. Several guys asked Elizabeth for a date, but she turned them down by saying she had to go back to Louisville. She told Donna that her visit had been a real boost for her ego, but she wasn't going to let it go to her head. Donna replied that it was time Elizabeth realized how attractive she was and to start trusting men again. Elizabeth said, "I have to take baby steps, but I'm trying."

Elizabeth landed a job with a prestigious, interior design firm a few weeks after she visited Donna. Although the job didn't pay much, she loved it because she was able to use her artistic talent when she worked on interior designs for wealthy clients. Her detailed sketches allowed clients to visualize how their new designs would look when completed. She received many compliments on her work and her self-esteem grew.

Elizabeth occasionally dated but never let herself to become attached to any of the men she dated. She desperately wanted to meet a special man and have a serious relationship. Sadly, most of the men were just looking for a good time. She had no desire to sleep with any of them and always moved on after a few dates when they became more obvious about their intentions.

CHAPTER 22

During the next few years, Donna and Elizabeth visited each other often. Most of their girlfriends from college were either married or getting married. Both of them longed for a special man, but neither had found one. Their similar situations created an even stronger bond of friendship and understanding.

Donna called Elizabeth and said she was coming to Louisville and hoped to spend the weekend. Without much enthusiasm, Elizabeth said it would be good to get together. Donna's radar went up when she heard the tone of Elizabeth's voice. She knew something was wrong but decided to wait until she got to Louisville to find out what was going on.

When Donna arrived Friday afternoon for the weekend, Elizabeth's friend Laura greeted her at the door. "Thank goodness you're here. Elizabeth has been crying for a week and won't get out of bed. She's been drinking a lot this week, too."

"What happened? I thought she sounded really down on the phone, but I didn't ask her what was going on."

"She lost her job because the design firm lost a couple of big contracts, and I think there's also something that happened with a man."

Donna was more concerned about the man than she was about the job. She knew she couldn't help with the job, but she knew she could help with man troubles. "What man? She didn't tell me she was seriously dating anyone."

Laura yelled out to Elizabeth from the kitchen, "Elizabeth, Donna is here. Now get up and wash your face." While Elizabeth was in the bathroom, Laura and Donna sat in the small kitchen and discussed what brought Elizabeth to this point. Laura said, "Elizabeth has been spiraling into a depression for weeks, and losing her job was the final straw. She went out a few times with an attorney but she hasn't seen him for weeks. I don't know what happened. She won't talk about it! See if you can find out and get her to cheer up. She needs to get her act together and find another job".

"I'll find out what's going on. She always tells me everything. I'll do my best to cheer her up." Laura hugged Donna and left.

Donna suspected that the situation with the attorney might be similar to what happened with Gary. She knew that Elizabeth had never completely gotten over how things ended with Gary, but she didn't say anything to Laura about her suspicions. Elizabeth had never told Laura anything about what happened with Gary, and Donna wasn't going to betray her confidence. *That jerk will never know the damage he caused.*

Elizabeth walked into the kitchen and announced that she wanted to go to a local bar. Donna tried to lighten the mood, "Let's go out and drink heavily. I can't wait to hear what's been going on." Elizabeth didn't say anything as she gathered her purse and coat.

It was early evening when Elizabeth and Donna walked into the bar. The evening crowd had not arrived so the bar was almost empty. Music blared from the sound system and they chose a table at the front of the bar and away from the speakers. When the waitress arrived to take their order, Donna ordered a glass of wine and Elizabeth ordered a Vodka Gimlet. *Oh, Lord, this is serious. I've never seen Elizabeth drink hard liquor before.* Over their drinks, Donna told Elizabeth everything that was going on in her life. She didn't ask Elizabeth what was wrong because she knew Elizabeth would get to it eventually.

After they ordered the second round, Elizabeth finally told Donna what happened. She had been dating a prominent attorney who became overly possessive after a few dates. "We were at a party. I started talking to some guy who was standing next to me while he went to get us some drinks. He came back and screamed at me in front of everybody. I freaked out! You know me. I hate it when someone I'm with causes a scene. Everyone stared at us and I was really embarrassed. He literally dragged me out of the party and screamed at me all the way home. Then the S.O.B. dumped me off at the sidewalk in front of my apartment. He never called back but I wouldn't have gone out with him if he did. I can't stand control freaks! Not since Gary. Then, without any warning, I was out of a job. I did the only thing I could think of--I stayed in bed drunk for a week."

Donna laughed and said that she couldn't have come up with a better plan. Elizabeth seemed so fragile that Donna did everything she could think of during the weekend to cheer her up. They went to the movies, to lunch, dinner, and visited several of the local bars. When Donna was getting ready to leave on Sunday afternoon, Elizabeth said she felt much better. She was going out the next day to find a new job and to begin painting again.

Elizabeth joked, "After I find a job, I'm going to find someone who's not a control freak. I can't stand being with someone who's possessive and critical. I just want someone who loves me and makes me feel secure. I'm not going to spend my life walking on egg shells. I know there has to be a man out there who's not a control freak or just looking for a good time. That's not too much to ask from life. Is it?"

Donna hugged her, "It's not. Good luck finding one. If you do, ask if he has a single friend." They both laughed.

On her way home, Donna decided that Elizabeth was going to be okay. Maybe dating another self-centered, control freak would push her to look for a different type of man. Elizabeth needed a man who adored her more than he adored himself.

CHAPTER 23

A group of young entrepreneurs had purchased a three-story, brick home as an investment and had converted each floor into an apartment to pay their mortgage. Elizabeth loved the old house as soon as she saw it and quickly signed a lease for the third-floor apartment. Elizabeth's apartment had one bedroom, a kitchen, a tiny bathroom, and a small living room. The best things about the apartment were the working fireplace and tall windows. Her father grumbled about how often they had to move her furniture while he was trying to get her piano up the stairs. Even with two other men helping, it was a difficult task.

Giving the family piano to Elizabeth had been her mother's idea. Elizabeth always played the piano when she visited her parents' and she was thrilled when her mother offered to give it to her. When the piano was finally in place, her father declared that she had to live in that apartment for the rest of her life because he wasn't going to move her again. He joked that he was glad she had a year's lease because it would take him that long to recover from this move. She hugged her dad and promised she would stay there at least a year, but she couldn't guarantee that she wouldn't move again. She decorated the apartment with her paintings and arranged a small area for her work space to paint near one of the tall windows in the living room. She liked the apartment better than any she had before because, as she said, it had character. Although she was generally happy, she was lonely living by herself.

Donna came to visit for a weekend. As she approached the apartment's door, she could hear Elizabeth playing Elton John's tribute to Marilyn Monroe, *Candle in the Wind*. She stood in the hallway and listened until Elizabeth finished the song before knocking. Elizabeth hugged Donna as she entered the apartment and said, "How long were you out there? I didn't hear you knock."

Donna always marveled at Elizabeth's seemingly unlimited talent. She played the piano with as much passion as she painted. "I waited until you were finished with the song. I loved hearing you play. I took lessons for years and I can't play Chopsticks. You are so talented. You can sing, play the piano, and paint. I do well to walk across the room without falling down." Elizabeth laughed and said, "I'm not that good. I just love to play."

After Donna settled in, Elizabeth showed her the painting she was painting to give Trisha for her birthday. On a pale green background, she had painted a bare tree with many branches. Roses, carnations, lilies, and daisies hung from the branches. The painting was amazing. Donna was impressed with how much Elizabeth's talent had grown over the last few years.

Donna pouted and said, "I feel left out. Trisha gets a picture and I want a picture! After all, I've known you longer." Elizabeth laughed and promised to paint one for her someday. They had a great weekend together, but it would be a while until they would see each other again because they were both busy with their jobs and were dating most weekends.

CHAPTER 24

Residents in one of the other old homes down the street from Elizabeth's apartment house decided to throw a block party in honor of Oktoberfest. They put up fliers to advertise the neighborhood party. Each building on the block was responsible for providing a keg of beer and snacks. The weather cooperated and it was a beautiful, crisp, fall evening on the night of the party. Word quickly spread beyond the neighborhood and several hundred people milled around sidewalks and yards.

Elizabeth stood next to the beer keg in front of her building while she chatted with one of her neighbors. A man, close to her age, walked between them and excused himself for interrupting as he filled his cup with a fresh beer. She glanced at him. He was about her height with a stocky build, jet-black hair, and piercing, ice-blue eyes. *Very attractive!*

He introduced himself. "Hi, my name is Bill and I tagged along with my cousin Larry to the party. He lives in an apartment in one of the houses down the street. Having a block party is a great idea." He looked Elizabeth up and down and asked, "Who are you? You look just like Natalie Wood. Can I get you a beer?"

"Yes, thank you."

"Why so formal? I won't bite." Bill said as he flashed his best smile.

Elizabeth immediately felt at ease with him. *Charming and handsome. Wow!* Bill retrieved a cup, filled it with beer, and handed it to her. "It was nice to meet you. By the way, I didn't catch your name."

"Elizabeth."

"Nice to meet you, Elizabeth. See you later." He smiled and then strolled away to join Larry, who was standing in the next yard.

During the course of the evening, she stole glances at Bill. Each time, he was looking back at her. Around nine, she decided it was time to go home because the party was getting rowdy. She began to make her way to the front door of her building when she felt a hand on her shoulder and turned to see Bill smiling at her.

"Let's go somewhere to get a cup of coffee so we can get to know each other."

Elizabeth only thought about it for a second and then agreed. She suggested they walk down the block to a small café. She didn't know him and she wasn't going to get in a car with him even though she had felt an instant attraction to him.

Chapter 25

The café was dimly lit and furnished with groupings of overstuffed couches and coffee tables. The comfortable seating encouraged patrons to linger over their coffee and read or chat with friends. When they walked in, the scent of brewing coffee and cigarettes filled the air. Elizabeth chose a loveseat positioned along the back wall. The waitress arrived almost immediately and asked how they wanted their coffee. Elizabeth said she preferred hers black. Bill smiled and said, "Make that two". They fell into an easy conversation.

Bill said, "I'm taking classes for a degree in history and I want to eventually become an attorney. I may even run for office someday. What about you?"

Elizabeth described her mundane job working at an art gallery but explained that she wanted to stay connected to art in some way. She told him that she dreamed of getting good enough to sell her work and maybe go to Paris someday. Bill talked about his conservative, political views. Although Elizabeth thought of herself as a liberal, she found herself agreeing with much of what he had to say. He was obviously very intelligent in addition to being handsome.

After an hour of nonstop talking, Bill said, "You're not what I expected. I thought you'd be a real stuck-up snob, being so beautiful and all. But you aren't, you're really nice."

His compliment made her blush, "I'm not comfortable around people I don't know and I'm not very outgoing in a crowd of people. I guess I'm shy. People often mistake my shyness for snobbery, or so I've been told. Thank you for giving me a chance. Most men don't."

Bill leaned over and quietly said, "I need a joint. Would you care to join me?"

Elizabeth laughed and said, "I haven't smoked pot since I was in college. Well, of course, lead the way."

As they left the café, Bill asked where they should go. He explained he didn't have a key to Larry's apartment and finding him in the crowd might be a problem. She decided he was safe and suggested they go back to her apartment. As they walked to her apartment, she thought he was not like other men she had dated and maybe that was a good thing.

Bill settled onto Elizabeth's couch and produced a joint. He lit it, took a hit, and offered it to her. She laughed at his jokes and felt free to challenge some of his opinions. She and Bill talked into the wee hours of the night. Around three, she suggested that Bill spend the night because he wouldn't want to wake Larry to get into the apartment. Acting as a gentleman should, Bill stretched out on the couch.

During the course of the evening, he hadn't tried to put the moves on her but she found herself wanting him. He was the first guy since Gary with whom she had even thought about having a physical relationship. She decided it was time to take the plunge. She stood smiling in her bedroom door and said, "You don't have to sleep on the couch." He immediately jumped off the couch and followed her into the bedroom.

Chapter 26

When Bill saw Elizabeth at the block party, he decided he had to meet her. She was beautiful, but he figured she must be stupid, because how often is a woman both beautiful and smart? He enjoyed playing mind games with stupid women. Much to his surprise, she was not just beautiful, she was highly intelligent and very sensitive, as well. When she invited him to her apartment, he was elated. Throughout that evening, he wanted her but he needed for her to make the first move because he could tell from the things she said that she didn't sleep around. He couldn't believe his luck when she invited him to spend the night. He thought it would take a while before he got her into bed.

* * * *

Elizabeth lit a candle in the bedroom and began to undress. Bill quickly undressed and took Elizabeth into his arms. Bill told her that she was beautiful and special. He took time to make sure she was pleasured and satisfied while they made love. Elizabeth found herself falling under his spell as they made love. She was glad she had taken a chance on him because he was tender, loving, and caring.

Over coffee the next morning, Bill said, "I don't want our time together to end. Lady, I don't know how it happened, but somewhere between the coffee last night and the coffee this morning, I've fallen in love with you."

Elizabeth was surprised by his comment. She didn't think he could possibly be in love with her, but it was really nice to know that he didn't consider her just a one-night stand. She tried to laugh off his comment by saying, "You're just in lust."

Bill knew that he had pushed too hard, "Go out with me tonight, and we'll take it slow and easy."

"Well, of course, sir, I would love to go out with you tonight."

When Bill got back to Larry's apartment, Larry teased him about getting lucky. Bill glared at him when he answered, "Yes, I got lucky and she is an amazing woman. I'm going to see her again. You'd better never tell her anything about me. If you do, I'll kill you. Are we clear?" Larry knew he meant it and promised he would never say anything.

During the next few weeks, Elizabeth and Bill saw each other every day. He learned just how emotionally delicate she really was when she opened up and told him how deeply she had been hurt by a guy she dated in college. He also learned she hated an overly-jealous and controlling man. Bill used all of this newfound information to his advantage. Although it enraged him anytime he saw her talk to another man, he kept his feelings to himself. He was an expert in hiding his true feelings and thoughts.

He did everything he could to make her fall in love with him. Every day, he told her how beautiful she was and he kissed her hello anytime they had been apart. She found herself thinking about him all the time and looked forward to spending time with him. She loved his wit and his intelligence and the fact that he wasn't critical, possessive, or jealous. He didn't try to change her and seemed to be sincere when he told her how much he cared for her. She knew she was falling in love with him although she admitted to herself that it was a different kind of love than what she had with Gary. This was a safe and comfortable love. For the first time in her life, she believed she could be herself with a man without fear of judgment.

During one of their conversations, she learned that he didn't believe in God and she was shocked. He thought God was a myth

71

created by man and Jesus was a nice guy who tricked the masses into believing he performed miracles. He argued that there was no scientific proof that a God exists and or that there is life after death. She tried to convince him otherwise, but he held fast to his position. She thought she could eventually convince him to believe and vowed never to give up on trying to save his soul.

After a few months of dating, Bill moved in with her. By that time, he was spending every night at her apartment anyway. She called Donna to tell her the news, but she kept her living arrangements from her parents. They wouldn't approve of her living with a man if she wasn't married. About the same time, Bill moved in with Elizabeth, Larry bought a small farm about an hour away from Louisville.

CHAPTER 27

Bill loved the way people looked at him when he went out with Elizabeth. Men were envious and women seemed to be more interested in him. He began to believe that having her in his life would ensure that he would rise to greatness one day. He cared more about how he felt when he was with her than he cared about her, but he never let her see that side of his personality. He continued to take classes to get his degree so that he could go to law school. Having Elizabeth by his side would guarantee his success and the sky was the limit.

* * * *

A year went by and Elizabeth took a job as a high school art teacher. The money was good and the hours were better than she had at the art gallery. She didn't have to work weekends and she had holidays and summers off with pay. She really enjoyed bringing out the undeveloped, artistic talents in her students. Bill worked at a local bookstore to bring in extra money while he finished his degree. Her life wasn't very exciting but she was content and happy.

Larry's dog had a litter of puppies in the spring after Bill moved in with Elizabeth. They went to the farm to see the puppies and to visit Larry. Elizabeth couldn't resist the cute, cuddly creatures. She rolled around on the ground and played with them while Bill and Larry talked. When they got ready to leave, she begged Bill for a puppy. He really didn't want a dog, but he wasn't going to say "No" if she wanted one so badly. She picked the runt of the litter and named him Red. She held Red in her lap on the ride home and kept thanking Bill for letting her have him. Bill realized that agreeing to have a dog had gotten him major points. He could put up with the dog because it was one more thing that bound her to him. As soon as they got home, Bill went out and bought dog food, a collar and leash, and several dog toys. She believed that Bill really loved the dog. That night, Red slept on the floor on her side of the bed and he didn't have an accident in the house or chew on anything other than his toys, ever. He was a perfect dog and having Red made her feel like they were a real family.

CHAPTER 28

After Red came to live with them, Elizabeth began to drop hints about getting married. She didn't come right out and say that that's what she wanted, but Bill knew that marriage was the next, logical step. He loved her as much as he could ever love anyone, and he knew he would never let her go. There was only one reason he could think of that would prevent them from getting married. He had to tell her about his past, but he was going to make sure that he did it in a way that didn't scare her away.

One snowy, Saturday night, Bill and Elizabeth sat in front of the fireplace enjoying a glass of wine. He decided it was time to tell her about his past. His tone was serious when he said, "I need to tell you something."

"Okay, you know you can tell me anything." *I just hope I can handle it. If there's another woman, I'll go crazy.*

He dove into the story he had concocted, "My father is not a smart man, but he thinks he knows everything. My mother is a wimp who won't stand up to him. When I was young, I got into arguments with my father all the time. I didn't mean to, but I made him look stupid any time we argued and he hated me for that. We lived in an old, rundown, farmhouse at the time. One day, I accidentally knocked over a burning candle and the curtains caught fire. I tried to put the fire out but the old house was a tinderbox. Everyone got out, but the house was a total loss. My father used the fire as an excuse to get rid of me. He lied and said that I started the fire on purpose. I was sent to juvenile detention until I was eighteen. While I was there, I was forced to take drugs. All of the boys were. Using drugs to control the boys in the detention center was standard practice at that time. I hated the drugs because they made me feel like a zombie. When I arrived there, I hated my parents for what they had done to me. By the time I got out, I realized that hating them wasn't worth my emotional energy because they are just pathetic people. I've come to terms with all of it but I'll never be close to them. I've never told anyone else about this, and I believe you need to know everything about me. Larry knows but he doesn't talk about it with anyone. I made him promise not to. Those memories are painful and I don't ever want to talk about this again after tonight."

Bill watched her carefully as he told his story. He wanted to be sure that she believed what he was saying.

"Bill! How horrible for you! In spite of all of that, you turned out great! I promise that I'll never bring it up again. I feel closer to you now because you trust me enough to share that with me. I know it must have been really hard for you to tell me about it. I love you and nothing you did in the past is going to change that. I was afraid you were going to tell me you were interested in another woman." The thought flitted through her mind that his horrible childhood explained why he didn't believe in God. People who endure horrible things sometimes blame God or stop believing altogether. She vowed she would try harder to bring him to believe in God.

Good, she bought it. He kissed her deeply, "I'll never be interested in another woman, and I love you more than life itself."

CHAPTER 29

They went out for a celebration dinner at an upscale, romantic restaurant the evening Bill graduated from college. Smooth jazz played in the background and trees were decorated with twinkling lights, completing the romantic setting. Bill ordered a bottle of champagne to celebrate. When the champagne was poured, he looked deeply into Elizabeth's eyes and said, "Let's make this a real celebration. I love you so much. I want you to be my wife. Will you marry me?"

Elizabeth thought they would eventually get married but she hadn't expected him to ask her that night. "Yes!" she exclaimed without hesitation.

Bill leaned over and kissed her. The kiss was a pre-arranged signal for the waiter to bring a small plate with an oyster shell on it and place it in front of Elizabeth. She was stunned when she saw that a diamond ring was lying in the shell. Bill picked up the ring, put it on her finger, and kissed her again. She was completely surprised by his thoughtfulness in making his proposal so special. The diamond was small. But, to Elizabeth, it was the most beautiful ring she had ever seen. After they kissed, they clicked their champagne glasses to toast their new life together. Bill reached for her hand and held it tightly. "I promise to always love you and keep you safe and secure. You are my life. You've made me the happiest man in the world by saying you will be my wife!" Bill knew that love and security were what Elizabeth wanted most from life and he believed he could keep that promise. He also knew that he had scored major points for the way he asked her to marry him.

Bill wanted to get married at City Hall, but she wanted a church wedding. She said she wanted to be married in the eyes of God, but he thought that it was a bunch of hogwash. He was going to argue with her, but he decided to let her have her way because it didn't matter to him where they got married. All he cared about was making sure that she belonged to him for the rest of his life.

Elizabeth couldn't wait to call Donna with the news and to ask her to be a bridesmaid at the wedding. Donna readily accepted, "I am so happy for you! Of course, I'll be in your wedding. This will make five weddings I have been in. I'm going broke paying for bridesmaid's dresses, but who cares. You're getting married and I wouldn't miss it for the world! 'Always a bridesmaid. Never a bride'." Elizabeth laughed and assured Donna that her time would come.

CHAPTER 30

Elizabeth and Bill moved into a two-bedroom apartment on the top floor of an old house after they became engaged. Bill asked some friends to move the furniture so Elizabeth would not have to ask her father to move her again. The apartment had a gas fireplace, and the building had a fenced-in courtyard where Red could run and play. A staircase in the apartment led to a small attic. Their landlord said that the attic came with the apartment and they were free to use it. Elizabeth converted the second bedroom into a studio for her painting and the attic into a study for Bill. He spent much of his time in the small, attic room. He read history books and smoked pot there while she painted, cooked dinner, or cleaned the apartment.

Elizabeth had no idea how much pot he was smoking, but she did notice that he spent more and more time in the attic. She occasionally smoked a little pot on weekends but usually stayed with just drinking wine. She was really happy that her life was so wonderful.

She began to run to get in shape for the wedding and to give Red more exercise. As her stamina grew, she was able to run three miles with ease. She always felt really calm for several hours after running. Elizabeth read somewhere that running released endorphins in the brain and they acted like tranquilizers. Getting a natural high was touted as a big benefit of running. She ran as often as she could because she felt the stress of planning a wedding and teaching.

One Saturday morning Elizabeth drove to Cherokee Park to run. Bill had taken Red to the vet for his yearly shots and she was running without him that day. About an hour into her run, she saw a man running toward her. As he drew closer, she realized it was Gary and she panicked! *What if he stops to talk? What will I say? How should I act?* She didn't have to worry because he ran past her. He looked directly at her but didn't even slow down. She ran faster for a few hundred feet and then she slowed down, ran in place, and looked back. He still ran away from her. She shook as she ran to the car. When she got home, she poured herself a glass of wine and smoked a joint.

* * * *

Gary realized that it was Elizabeth running toward him. *God, she looks great! Should I stop and speak to her? No, I'm married with kids and my wife is already suspicious that I am having an affair with my secretary. Maybe I'll just say hi. No, it's better to pretend that I didn't recognize her. I should never have let her go. I could have made it on my own without my father-in-law's money. How stupid was I? She was the best thing that ever happened to me.* He looked into Elizabeth's eyes as he ran past her. *She recognized me. I should have stopped. No, it's better that I didn't open that can of worms. I can't afford a divorce.*

CHAPTER 31

Elizabeth finally told her parents that she and Bill were living together. Although they didn't approve, they didn't say anything because she was getting married. Elizabeth invited Donna to spend the night after a shower her mother had thrown for her. Donna readily accepted because they hadn't been able to spend time together in ages. Bill went to Larry's that day and wouldn't come home until late that night. This gave the girls time to catch up without interruption. After they carried the shower presents into the apartment, Elizabeth poured two glasses of wine and sat down on the couch next to Donna. Red was stretched out in front of the fire and slept while they talked.

After they caught up on the latest gossip, their conversation took a very serious turn. Donna asked, "Elizabeth, are you really happy now?"

Elizabeth answered, "I am happy. I'm comfortable with Bill. It's not the same as it was with Gary. Bill is more like a companion. We never argue. He's good to me and I do love him."

Elizabeth took a deep breath and continued. She didn't look at Donna as she began the story. "There's one thing about Bill that no one knows. He told me that when he was thirteen, he accidentally burned down his family's house and was sent to a juvenile detention center to live until he was eighteen. He was forced to take medication while he was there." She repeated the entire story that Bill had told her, and she added, "Bill and his parents have made peace now, but they aren't close. I've only met them once. Larry is the closest thing to family that Bill has. I doubt that his parents will even come to the wedding."

Donna waited without responding. She sensed that there was more that Elizabeth needed to say. Elizabeth stared at the flames that danced in the fireplace as she continued.

"Bill smokes a lot of pot. He says that smoking pot is no different than drinking alcohol to relieve stress, and I guess he's right. We all need something. I run and drink wine. You won't believe this. One day, when I was running, I ran right past Gary. I know he recognized me but he didn't speak. It was as if I had been anyone he would run past. All of the hurt came flooding back and I was really shaken up after seeing him. In a funny way, it made me appreciate Bill even more. I feel secure with him and I know he loves me. He doesn't judge me and he doesn't have a jealous bone in his body. I realize now that I was never totally at ease with Gary. I always tried to please him but never myself. Bill loves me for me and doesn't want to change me. That's more important than being wildly in love like I was with Gary. So, yes, I am happy."

Donna thought Elizabeth sounded like she was trying to convince herself she made the right choice to marry Bill. When Elizabeth finished her story, she took a drink of her wine and finally looked at Donna, "What do you think?"

"That story about Bill burning down the house is scary. Are you sure that he is telling you the whole truth?"

"He has no reason to lie about it."

"Elizabeth, please don't marry him right now. You can live with him for a while longer. You know - just to be sure that he's okay. Could you ask Larry or would that be putting him in a bad place? If Bill did set the house on fire deliberately, that's a sign of a serious mental illness. You just said that you have met his parents only once. Maybe he doesn't want you around them. One of the drugs that I sell is an antipsychotic and we had to learn all about mental illness to sell it. In most cases, a psychotics' symptoms appear at the onset of puberty. Bill was thirteen, just hitting puberty, when the house was burned down. Sometimes mental illness disappears for years, but it always comes back. Please don't marry him until you can find out more about what happened when he was young." Donna realized she was begging Elizabeth not to marry Bill, but she felt that she had to speak from her heart this time.

Elizabeth shook her head, "I promised him that I would never bring it up again. I can't ask Larry because Bill would see that as a betrayal. I've never seen him out of control. In fact, he is the most controlled person I've ever met. His family probably did want to get rid of him. They're really odd people. His parents were cold and distant when I met them. I've never met his brother and sister because they live out of state. Bill says they're as weird as his parents and he doesn't keep in touch with them. I'm afraid that I'll lose him if I don't marry him now. I'm going through with it. Let's change the subject."

Donna knew Elizabeth well enough to know that she had made up her mind about marrying Bill. It wouldn't help to try to discuss it further.

She changed the subject by asking about Elizabeth's wedding dress. Grateful that Donna had dropped the subject, Elizabeth described her dress in great detail. They spent the rest of the evening talking about Elizabeth's wedding plans. When Bill came home around nine o'clock, he said, "Hi," to Donna and then went up to the attic. He didn't come down until after midnight.

As Donna drove home, she replayed the conversation over in her mind. The story about Bill burning down his family's house was terrifying. She was sure that there was more to it than Bill had said. *People just don't get rid of their kids because they're smartasses.* She wondered if Gary had just stopped to talk to Elizabeth, would she still be marrying Bill? *Damn that Gary. He could have at least said 'Hi'.*

CHAPTER 32

It was a beautiful, sunny, spring day when Elizabeth and Bill got married in a small, white, country church. The bridesmaids wore dresses of kelly-green, Elizabeth's favorite color. Larry was Bill's best man. None of Bill's family came to the wedding. Her father was misty eyed when he walked her down the aisle. Bill didn't close his eyes or bow his head during the prayers, but no one noticed. The picture of the wedding party was stunning. The little, white church in the background provided a perfect backdrop for the picture. Everyone was smiling in the picture, but Donna thought that Elizabeth's smile looked strained. She rationalized that *maybe Elizabeth was just tired. She's been overloaded with teaching and taking care of wedding details.*

Elizabeth and Donna kept in touch sporadically after the wedding. Elizabeth was getting her Masters' degree while teaching high school art. Bill had gone back to take education classes so that he could teach high school history. He still held out hope ,that he would one day become an attorney and a teaching job would provide the additional income they needed to pay for his law school tuition.

Elizabeth and Bill's schedules were so hectic that they decided to give Red back to Larry. It wasn't fair for Red to be cooped up all day in the apartment. At Larry's, he would be free to run on the farm. Although Elizabeth knew it was best for Red, she missed him terribly. He had become her constant companion, while Bill spent most of his time in the attic.

CHAPTER 33

It was 1979 and Donna decided to throw herself a 30th birthday party. The theme of the party was, 'Come dressed as your suppressed desire'. She was dating a new guy, Ed, and her birthday party would be a perfect time to introduce him to her friends. Naturally, Elizabeth and Bill were invited to the party. Elizabeth came dressed in an artist's smock and beret. Bill dressed in a suit, tie, and carried a briefcase. He came as an attorney.

Elizabeth painted a picture for Donna's birthday present. She began by painting a solid-black background on the canvas. She knew that Donna loved flowers, so she painted bright orange lilies on the black background. She worked on the painting for weeks and constantly changed it until each petal was complete with minute details. The flowers looked alive against the dark background. Elizabeth was never completely satisfied with the painting, but she couldn't figure out exactly what it was that she didn't like about it.

When she gave Donna the painting, Donna was thrilled. She hung the painting over her fireplace where everyone could see it. The next day, Donna was admiring the painting when Ed made the comment that although the painting was of bright orange flowers, it exuded a feeling of depression and desperation. Donna agreed, but said she didn't care because Elizabeth had painted it just for her and she loved the painting.

CHAPTER 34

Bill completed his college courses and landed a job teaching history in a local high school. He expected the teaching job would provide the money he needed for law school. Female students flocked to Bill's classes because he was so incredibly good looking. Male students loved Bill's classes because he made historical figures come alive through the stories he told. Overall, he was a great success as a teacher. His ego swelled as it fed off of the adoration from his students. He believed he was the best at everything he did.

Bill stopped smoking pot after he got the teaching job. He told Elizabeth that he quit because he didn't believe a teacher should use illegal drugs. Although things were going fine, Bill started to feel depressed and anxious. He told himself it was because he had to get a Master's in Education to continue to teach and that was going to cost money. Once again, law school would have to wait. He promised himself he would start law school as soon as he was finished with his Master's. With their combined income, they were able to pay for his Master's and still put some money away for his law school.

A couple of months before the lease on their apartment ended, Elizabeth started pushing Bill to buy a house. She was tired of living in an apartment and wanted permanent roots. She said, "Buying a house makes sense because a house payment would be close to what we're paying in rent. Why not build equity instead of making a landlord rich?"

Bill agreed because he was tired of living in an apartment, too. When they found the perfect little house in an older section of Louisville, her father came over to check out the plumbing and electrical fixtures before they bought it and said he couldn't find any major problems, but the heat pump would have to be replaced in a few years. They had to use all of the money they had saved for Bill's law school as a down payment on the small three-bedroom-house. She promised him they would replace the money as soon as possible.

Their little white house had a small backyard with a patio and a detached garage. The neighborhood was filled with young families and she thought it was perfect.

Sunday, after they moved into their house, they drove around the neighborhood to check it out. Children were playing in the yards and young mothers were pushing babies in strollers on almost every street in the neighborhood. She commented that it appeared as if their new neighborhood was perfect for raising a family. Bill ignored the comment.

Elizabeth was excited that she would finally be able to paint the walls colors that would showcase her paintings. The walls in their apartment had all been off white and did nothing to show off her paintings. She poured through magazines looking for decorating ideas and decided on a comfortable country decorative style. Her prior experience working in interior design helped her to decorate using the furniture they already had. She scoured second-hand furniture stores to find additional pieces they needed for their house. Elizabeth painted the living room a hunter green. The color accented her tweed couch and made the colors in her paintings pop. She painted the eat-in kitchen a sunny yellow. Her dishes were bright red. She found a real deal on an antique, roll-top desk and an overstuffed leather chair for the study. She painted the study walls chocolate brown and brightened the room by painting the bookcase orange. The room was inviting and functional when she finished it. She bought a used brass bed for the guest bedroom and painted its walls cherry red. Elizabeth was especially proud of how the master bedroom turned out. It was big enough to use a small white love seat and cherry table she found at the used furniture store to create a sitting area. She painted their bedroom deep, sky blue. Her mother bought a white, down-filled comforter as a housewarming present and it looked great against the blue walls. Her mother said the room looked heavenly. When she finally finished decorating, her house looked better than some of the pictures she had seen in the magazines. Everyone commented on how warm and inviting it was.

Bill liked the house well enough. He was glad to be out of the apartment, but he was upset that they had not been able to save any money for his law school since buying the house. In his opinion, Elizabeth had spent every free dime they had decorating the house. Utilities took a bigger chunk of their budget than they had spent at the apartment. He hoped that, now that the house was finished, they could start saving for his law school again. Elizabeth never knew he was upset about the money she spent to decorate the house. He kept those feelings to himself but his resentment continued to grow.

CHAPTER 35

Donna and Ed decided to marry in June of 1980. They bought a three-bedroom, split foyer house and moved into the house a few months before their wedding. Donna called Elizabeth to ask her to be in the wedding and Elizabeth readily agreed. "You'll finally get to be the bride and I know you'll be beautiful!" When she told Bill the news, he asked how much the bridesmaid dress was going to cost. She thought he was kidding and never gave it a second thought. He knew that being in a wedding was going to take another chunk of their money. They would have to pay for the dress, hotel room, bridal shower present, and wedding present. He knew Elizabeth would want to buy pictures of the wedding, too. He started thinking that Elizabeth only cared about her own wants and needs. He really resented it, but he kept his feelings to himself.

Elizabeth drove to Lexington to spend the weekend and to be fitted for her bridesmaid's dress. Donna had chosen a light pink, off-the-shoulder, chiffon dress that would look fabulous on her bridesmaids. She explained that she wanted a dress that her bridesmaids could wear again, if they went to a formal occasion. Elizabeth laughed at the idea that she would be going to any formal affairs. Her life as a teacher and wife did not include parties, or formal affairs. She joked, "My life is boring and normal. Just the way I want it".

Donna's wedding was beautiful. The photographer took a picture of each bridesmaid as she came down the aisle. All of the bridesmaids, except Elizabeth, were smiling. She had a haunted look in her picture. Donna thought the photographer should have gotten a better picture of Elizabeth. But, when she looked at all the pictures that included Elizabeth, she realized that Elizabeth looked the same in each picture. She couldn't shake the feeling that something wasn't right with Elizabeth. However, every time they talked, Elizabeth said she was happy with her life.

CHAPTER 36

A few months after Donna's wedding, Bill and Elizabeth drove to Lexington to spend the weekend with Donna and Ed. Bill didn't want to go, but Elizabeth insisted that they needed to get away for a weekend. Bill grumbled all the way to Lexington and said he would be bored the whole weekend.

Soon after arriving in Lexington, Bill was glad they had come to visit, too. The two couples were sitting in the comfortable, family room drinking wine when Donna mentioned that Ed had recently joined the Civil War Roundtable in Lexington. Bill knew he had found someone who shared his interest in history and asked questions about the club and its purpose. Ed told Bill about the interesting speakers the Roundtable brought in for their quarterly meetings and the antique guns and relics the members brought to the meetings. Their conversation spilled over to the subject of guns. Ed had many new and antique guns in his collection and he loved to talk about them.

Bill said, "I've been thinking about buying a gun. A new, indoor, gun range just opened in Louisville and it would be a great place to learn how to shoot."

Ed agreed, "I think that every household needs to have a gun, but gun owners need to know how to use them. Guns are not toys. I shoot as often as I can. I do all the work on my guns and I load my own bullets. Do you want to see my workshop? I set it up in the garage." Bill jumped at the chance.

Elizabeth said, "I don't like guns and I don't want one in my house. Too many accidents can happen with guns." Donna thought, *I don't want to get into that conversation. It will never end.*

Donna announced that if Ed and Bill were going to play with guns, she and Elizabeth were going to make dinner. As Elizabeth and Donna walked to the kitchen, they passed Elizabeth's painting hanging in the living room. Elizabeth stopped and looked at the painting.

She said, "Wow, I didn't realize how dark and foreboding the painting is. I must have really been depressed when I painted it. Funny, I don't think I was depressed. Let me take it back and redo it."

"Not on your life! I want to keep it just as you painted it. Besides, I might never get it back and I love that painting. I think of you every time I look at it."

When Bill and Elizabeth left the next day, they promised to get together again soon.

CHAPTER 37

Soon after their visit with Donna and Ed, Bill's personality began to change. Every time he and Elizabeth went to the grocery store, he complained about the cost of food. When the utility bills came in, he complained about their rising costs. Elizabeth tried to appease him by buying inexpensive food like pasta and rice. He complained about never having steak every time she cooked a casserole. She clipped coupons to save money so that she could buy steak more often. She kept a close eye on the thermostat to try to save money on the electric bills, but he constantly changed the thermostat to a temperature that increased their monthly bill. She stopped buying new clothes and started shopping at second-hand stores. She had her hair cut at a beauty school and stopped buying department store makeup. It didn't matter what she did. He was angry all the time! She put as much money into savings as possible hoping that they would soon have enough for him to start law school and then he wouldn't be angry all the time.

In the fall of 1981, his mood brightened, but he didn't stop complaining about the money she spent. When the heat pump went out and they had to use all of their savings to pay for a new one, he threw a fit. He said that if she hadn't wanted the stupid house, they would have a ton of money. By the spring of the next year, not only was he not worried about saving money, he was spending money too freely. He bought himself an expensive leather coat and jewelry for Elizabeth. She loved the jewelry but asked him not to buy her any more presents because they almost didn't have enough money left to pay their mortgage payment. He exploded and called her ungrateful.

By the end of the summer, his spending spree ended but they were almost out of money.

They went to her parents' house for a Sunday evening dinner just before school started. Bill and Elizabeth's father were watching television in the den. She prepared a plate of snacks and went into the den. When Bill excused himself to use the bathroom, she said very quietly, "I don't want Mother to know about this, but Bill has been spending money like crazy for the last couple of months. We almost weren't able to pay the mortgage. He bought me several pieces of expensive jewelry and a leather jacket for himself. Although I love the jewelry, we can't afford to be spending money like that. I told him to stop and he finally did. I'm worried that he may start again. I don't know why I'm telling you this now. I guess I need to talk to someone about it."

Her father was careful with his answer because he didn't want to meddle too deeply into her affairs. "If I were you, I would keep a stash of money saved somewhere he doesn't know about. Just start putting a little aside each month and build a nest egg so that you have it if you need it. You've always been good with your money, and I don't want to see you get into a financial jam. You know you can always ask me for money if you need it. But, just for your peace of mind, squirrel some of your own money away." He pulled out his wallet and gave her the money he had. He winked at her when he handed her the money.

"Thanks, Dad, I knew you would know what to do." He smiled and hugged her. "Don't worry, I won't tell your mother about this." After talking with her father, Elizabeth started hiding any change she got back when she paid cash. She also always managed to find a little money every month to add to her stash. She kept it hidden in a sewing basket on the top shelf of the closet in their bedroom.

By the time Christmas rolled around, Bill was in a dark mood again. She came home with some presents she had gotten for her family, and he threw a fit about how much money she was spending. When she tried to explain that the presents were on sale, he slammed her against the wall and threatened to 'knock her into next year' if she talked back to him again. She was shocked and ran into the bedroom crying. He left and didn't come back until late that night.

As she sat in their bedroom and cried, she tried to understand what was happening to their marriage. She focused on the things he had blamed on her. *I wanted the house and it is costing us more in utilities and repairs than I thought it would. I wasn't grateful enough when he gave me the jewelry. I know he likes steak and I don't buy it often enough. I didn't ask him how much we could spend on Christmas presents. I haven't been able to save any money and he can't go to law school because of it.* Her self-esteem was low and getting lower as she accepted the blame for everything wrong in their lives. She vowed to try to be a better wife.

Bill stormed out of the house after he shoved her into the wall. *How dare she talk to me that way? She has no right. She bitched at me when I spent money and now it's supposed to be okay when she does!* He drove to a local bar and nursed a beer until he cooled down. He thought he was justified in putting her in her place.

By the time he got home, she was asleep and he didn't wake her. The next morning, she said it was her fault because she hadn't asked him how much she could spend on presents. He told her he forgave her and that cemented her belief that she was at fault.

Even though she was careful with the money she spent, they weren't able to save much money over the next few years. It seemed as if every time they thought they could put some extra money away, they needed to get something repaired or needed to buy a new appliance. Her old car and his old truck were constantly breaking down.

When her car needed another repair, they decided to stop throwing money into that bottomless pit and buy a new one. She picked out an inexpensive, blue compact with low, monthly payments. She picked the least expensive car on the lot so that they wouldn't have to use much of their limited savings on the down payment.

When they got home with her new car, Bill said that he needed to run to the drugstore. He took his truck instead of the new car when he left. When he came home, not only did he have a new truck, it was the most expensive truck on the lot. He had used all of their savings as a down payment and the monthly payments were double the payments of Elizabeth's car. She was shocked that he bought the new truck without discussing it with her first and told him so. He slapped her across her face and called her a selfish bitch. She immediately apologized for saying anything and told him he deserved a new truck.

Elizabeth didn't blame him for losing control. He had always given her anything she wanted. But, when he bought something for himself, she questioned it. She believed that she deserved to be punished for being so selfish--not slapped--but certainly be put in her place. *I need to be more supportive. I need to be a better wife. He's a good husband and he deserves to be happy.* She didn't realize that every time she accepted the blame, her ability to stand up to him was getting weaker and her self-esteem was sinking lower. She asked God to help her be a better wife.

CHAPTER 38

Elizabeth talked about having a baby, and Bill said he did want children but not until he completed law school. She didn't think he was ever going to be able to go to law school because the car and truck payments were making them live from paycheck to paycheck.

Every time Elizabeth mentioned having a baby, it made him angry. He knew that if she got pregnant his law school would have to wait yet again. He was depressed again and blamed it on her nagging about money and having a baby.

In June, Elizabeth decided she needed to get off of the pill because she heard it would take months or even years to get pregnant after she stopped taking them. She was sure that she could convince Bill that it was time to have a baby. She was still waiting for the right time to tell him when she had missed her period in July. She wasn't sure if she had missed her period because her body was adjusting to not taking the pill or if she was pregnant. She went to her doctor and he confirmed that she was pregnant. She was thrilled to be pregnant but afraid of what Bill would say about it. On the way home from the doctor's office, she said a prayer and asked God to let the baby be healthy. Also, she prayed to God to help her be a better wife because she felt guilty that she had stopped taking the pill without telling Bill.

On Friday night, after her doctor confirmed that she was pregnant, Bill poured two glasses of wine for them to drink while dinner was cooking. She had to tell him.

"I can't drink that."

"Why not? It's the same wine we always drink."

"Pregnant women aren't supposed to drink."

Bill was stunned and really angry but he knew it was too late to do anything about it. "How? When?" was all he said. She explained that she had stopped taking the pill in June. "I was going to tell you but I got pregnant before I had a chance. I thought it would take months or years before I got pregnant." He gulped the wine in his glass and then gulped the wine from Elizabeth's glass. She mistook his silence for acceptance.

As Elizabeth happily continued talking about having a baby, Bill tried to work through his feelings about this new development. *We don't need a baby now but she will never have an abortion. I haven't even started law school and a baby will ruin everything. I can't believe the bitch did this to me. On the other hand, having a baby will shut her up and I'm sick of her whining. Our health insurance will pay for the delivery and prenatal visits. If we're careful with our money, I can still go to law school and law firms like family men. Maybe having a baby now isn't such a bad idea after all.* He bought Elizabeth a dozen roses the next day.

He sank into a deeper depression after her announcement. He tried to work through why he was depressed by analyzing his situation. *Getting ready for the baby is taking Elizabeth's free time and she doesn't pay any attention to me. She's spending all of her time fixing up the nursery and reading baby books. All she ever talks about is the baby. We rarely go out anymore. Once the baby comes, we'll never be able to go anywhere. Teaching school is a bitch. Those kids don't want to learn and I hate the endless paperwork. No wonder I'm depressed. Who wouldn't be in the same situation? I need something to take my mind off things. I wish I could think of something to do to occupy my time while Elizabeth is nesting.*

In September, Bill was in the middle of a lecture on the right to bear arms when a student asked him what kind of guns he owned. He told the class that he had a few antique rifles because he didn't want to look like a hypocrite. At that moment, he decided to buy a gun and take lessons. He had been meaning to get one since talking with Ed anyway. Joining a gun club would get him out of the house and be a practical use of their money.

That night he told Elizabeth he was going to buy a gun. She was adamant that she didn't want a gun in the house. He argued, "Ed is right that every household needs a gun. And, if you own a gun, you have to know how to use it. I can join the gun club at the range and take lessons. It won't cost much. When it was just you and me, I figured you would be able to take care of yourself if anything ever happened. A baby is helpless and I want to be able to protect my family. We might need to have a gun to protect the baby someday." He thought that she really couldn't argue with that logic. Surprisingly, Elizabeth said, "You're right, we do need a gun for protection and you'll enjoy taking lessons. I think it's a great idea." Bill thought that his brilliant argument had persuaded her.

Elizabeth had been feeling guilty about getting pregnant. She noticed how depressed he was after her announcement. He hadn't helped with getting the nursery ready, and he never offered to go to the doctor with her. Buying a gun was the first thing he had shown any interest in since she told him about the baby. She hoped a new hobby would make him happy. If he really was going to take lessons, she wouldn't mind having a gun in the house.

During the next few months, Bill came out of his depression and started to take an interest in preparing for the baby. He brought home a book of baby names, and they spent hours looking up names and deciding combinations of names they liked. He believed a name could shape the baby's future, and he wanted his baby to have the right name. He teased her by saying that an appropriate name for a boy was Curly Moe and a baby girl should definitely be called Betty Crocker. They thought about using family names but decided that they wanted their baby to have its very own name. Bill said he liked Thomas Peter for a boy because he could be called Tom, Tommy, or Pete and he thought it sounded like a strong manly name. He picked Angela Leigh because he thought the name sounded lyrical and was a perfect name for a beautiful girl. Elizabeth agreed with his choices in the hopes that if he named the baby, he would feel closer to it.

CHAPTER 39

Elizabeth waited for a few months to tell anyone outside of her immediate family that she was pregnant. She called Donna in October to tell her the news and Donna was thrilled for her. Elizabeth shared the details of what she was doing to get ready for the baby. "I changed the guest bedroom into a nursery. Mom gave me a crib and Laura gave me her rocking chair. I painted the walls light green. We don't know the baby's sex because we decided we want to be surprised when it arrives. I painted lambs, kittens, and puppies on the walls." Donna could hear the delight in Elizabeth's voice as she described the nursery.

"Have you decided on a name yet?"

Elizabeth responded, "If it's a boy, we're going to name him Thomas Peter. If it's a girl, we're going to name her Angela Leigh. I can hardly wait to meet whoever it is."

Donna teased, "Looks like you have everything covered. I just changed companies and now I'm traveling all the time. I promise to come to see you when the baby arrives."

"I miss you."

"I miss you, too. Now, go and eat some pickles and ice cream." Elizabeth was laughing when she hung up.

CHAPTER 40

Elizabeth had a beautiful little girl on April Fool's Day. When the doctor pronounced the baby healthy and perfect, she said a prayer aloud, thanking God for giving her a beautiful and healthy baby. Bill started taking pictures while she was praying.

They named the baby Angela Leigh as planned. Angela had lots of curly, black hair and beautiful blue eyes, just like Bill. Bill felt on top of the world when Angela was born. Elizabeth laughed at the way he carried on about Angela and she told him that he was acting as if he was the first new father in the world. He took so many pictures of Angela in the nursery that Elizabeth's father kidded him that he should own stock in Kodak. He bought the most expensive cigars he could find and gave them to anyone who happened to walk by the nursery. She had no idea, at the time, how much he spent on film, development, and cigars. She found out when the monthly bills were due and they were almost out of money. Luckily, her parents had given her several hundred dollars to buy things for Angela, so she was able to cover the bills without saying anything to him about their shortfall. She told herself that he had just been overly excited about his new baby girl and didn't realize how much he had spent.

Through the years, Elizabeth had tried unsuccessfully to convert Bill into believing in God and Jesus. The last time she brought it up, he told her she was stupid to believe in a Supreme Being, and he didn't want to listen to her stupidity. When Angela was a month old, Elizabeth wanted to have her baptized in her family's church. Bill said, "There is no need to baptize the child because there is no God and baptizing is just a stupid ritual."

Elizabeth thought, *Angela's soul is at stake and I will stand up to him and raise her in the Christian faith. I'm at fault for the things wrong in our marriage but I am not backing down on this. She needs to know God's love and that he sent his son to earth to save us from our sins. I WILL NOT give in on this.*

She said, "Bill, I try to do everything I can to please you and to let you have your way, but this is different. Angela's soul is at stake and you will not stop me from having her baptized! I will not give in on this, so you better get used to the idea! Our child will be raised as a Christian and will believe in God."

Bill saw the defiant look in her eyes and was surprised because she never stood up to him. He knew that she was serious and even if he got physical with her, she would not back down. He didn't feel like having a fight anyway. He said, "If baptizing Angela is so important to you, go ahead and do it. Just don't expect me to be there for the stupid ritual." She took that as a sign that he might be softening his position about God. He wasn't.

Bill believed there was no God and baptizing Angela wouldn't make a difference in the long run. When Angela was old enough to understand things, he would explain that there is no scientific proof that God exists, and religions came into being as a means for ancient kings to keep people under control. She would be smart enough to know he was right. His daughter wasn't to believe in stupid myths.

He went to visit Larry the day Angela was baptized. When Elizabeth's parents asked where he was, she lied and said that Larry had some sort of emergency at the farm and needed Bill's help. She added to the lie by saying that Bill didn't want to postpone the baptism. She couldn't bring herself to tell them that the father of her child didn't believe in God. They would be horrified. While she was in the church, she silently prayed to God to forgive her for lying to her parents, and to touch Bill's heart, and to make him believe.

CHAPTER 41

Angela was a happy baby who rarely cried. It was obvious, early on, that she was going to be a real beauty and very intelligent. Bill and Elizabeth adored her. Instead of coming between them, Angela brought them closer. He was feeling on top of the world, and Elizabeth thought that his happiness came from having Angela. She didn't feel guilty anymore about having stopped taking the pill.

She was on maternity leave for the rest of the school year and then was home with Angela throughout the summer. As time for school to start drew near, she knew she had to find a daycare for Angela. Her heart was breaking because she would have to go back to work and leave her baby with a stranger. She checked out all of the daycare centers in the area and chose one that was located just a few miles out of their way traveling to and from their schools. It was the best in the area, but it was also very expensive. Elizabeth began to explain her choice and Bill started to object to how much it was going to cost, but she kept talking. He had stopped his lavish spending and was now being careful about how they spent their money.

"The daycare center only allows six children at a time. Mary, who runs the daycare, limits the number so she can give each child individual attention and she's certified in early childhood development. A spot just opened up because someone with a baby was transferred out of Louisville or we wouldn't be able to get her in there. I would rather stay at home and take care of Angela but we both know that's not possible. Everyone I've talked to says that Mary's daycare is one of the best in the whole city and we're lucky to be able to get in. I know it costs a lot but I want her to have the best. Don't you?"

"Of course, I want her to have the best! I know you want to stay home with her and I'm sorry that you can't. If I was already an attorney, we wouldn't be having this conversation. I guess Mary's daycare sounds like it is our best option. Call Mary and tell her we definitely will enroll Angela."

Elizabeth knew the instant he mentioned being a lawyer that he was still blaming her for keeping him from fulfilling his dream. She also knew there was nothing she could do about it but another wave of guilt sweep through her.

* * * *

Once Elizabeth gave him the details about the daycare center, Bill was going to agree to it. However, he used the opportunity to make her feel guilty again. They hadn't been able to put any money into savings since having Angela because diapers, formula, clothes, and toys for her were expensive. Now, with the added cost of daycare, there was no way he could start law school for a few years and he knew it. He resented Elizabeth for keeping him from his dream and had no qualms about reminding her every chance he got.

* * * *

The next day, they took Angela to the daycare center to meet Mary. Elizabeth liked her immediately, but Bill grilled Mary on every aspect of the facility until he was satisfied that it was the best place for Angela. Mary gladly answered all of his questions because she was proud of her daycare.

Even as an infant, Angela seemed to learn things quickly. Mary gave her extra attention and taught her to recognize shapes and colors early on. Angela was more advanced for her age than any child Mary had ever had at her daycare. In just a few, short months, Mary came to love Angela as if she were her own.

Mary and Elizabeth got to know each other really well because Elizabeth always stayed to chat for a while when she picked Angela up after school. She wanted to know everything that happened in Angela's day. It wasn't unusual for her to spend thirty minutes each day talking about how Angela's day had gone. After Elizabeth worried that she was missing Angela growing up and Mary knew how she felt. She assured her that whatever Angela did during the day she would do it at home, too. Mary understood how hard it is for working mothers to leave their babies and she sympathized with them. It had been hard for her to leave her own babies when her husband left her high and dry and she had to go to work.

Bill didn't pick up Angela often, but on the rare occasions when he did, he didn't stay to chat. Mary prided herself on being a good judge of character and she didn't care much for Bill. She confided to a friend that there was something just 'not right' about him, but she couldn't put her finger on it. He was always polite, smiling, and very appropriate. Nevertheless, she always felt uncomfortable when he picked up Angela. It finally dawned on her that she had never seen anyone so controlled.

Chapter 42

Shortly before Angela's first birthday, Bill became depressed again. He told himself that their tight finances were getting him down. He should have been a lawyer by now and they would have been on easy street. If she hadn't wanted a house and not had a baby, everything would be different. He believed that everything was Elizabeth's fault and constantly told her so. She was a few pounds heavier than she had been before the pregnancy, and he told her she looked frumpy. If her hair wasn't perfectly styled, he made nasty comments. Tearing her down made him feel better and he didn't care how much his comments hurt her.

Every time he blamed her for something, she became more willing to accept the blame and her self-esteem continued to diminish. On the rare occasions when Angela was fussy, Elizabeth took her into the nursery and shut the door so that Bill wouldn't be disturbed. She walked on eggshells around him all of the time. She took Angela to visit her parents or Laura every weekend just to get out of the house and away from Bill for a little while. She never let on that anything was wrong when she visited them. She believed that everything was her fault, and she couldn't bring herself to tell anyone what a terrible wife she was. Angela was the only bright spot in her life.

The Christmas before Angela's second birthday, Bill went on another spending spree. While he and Elizabeth were at a toy store, he wanted to buy more toys than Angela would ever be able to play with. Elizabeth tried to put some of the toys back and he screamed at her. Embarrassed, she ran out of the store and waited in the car. After she ran out, he added more toys to the cart, including a five-foot tall teddy bear that cost more than a hundred dollars.

Elizabeth had to secretly ask her father for money to get them through the month until their next paychecks arrived. Her father gave her the money, but he told her that he was worried about Bill's spending habits. She defended Bill by saying that he just wanted Angela to have the best Christmas ever. Her father let it go, but was worried that Bill's extravagant spending was a sign that something more serious was wrong with him.

When Bill slipped into another depression a few months later, she could tell that it was all he could do to get up and go to work. While he was at home, he slept most of the time. She tried to talk to him about it. He said, "The kids at school are driving me nuts. You, of all people, should know how bad teaching is. You're being an insensitive bitch. Just leave me alone." Once again, she felt horrible that she had upset him.

She knew that he went through periods of depressions when he slept all of the time. She also knew that sometimes he was 'super happy' and went days with only a few hours of sleep each night. The different sleep patterns occurred so far apart that she never thought they had anything to do with each other. Her biggest worry was that he was always angry about something she did or said. He never directed his anger toward Angela, which reinforced her belief that she was at fault.

She grew to hate the times when he didn't sleep much more than when he was depressed and sleeping most of the time when he wasn't working. In addition to his wild spending habits during those times, he constantly criticized her looks, was no longer affectionate, and had a wild look in his eyes. He was crude and rough when they made love. Elizabeth only objected once to the way he was treating her. That objection brought on a string of cruel comments which ended when he smashed a vase on her piano that put a big hole in the top of the piano. She covered the hole with a tablecloth runner so that no one would see it and ask questions. Just when she thought she couldn't take it any longer, he would ease up for a while and act fine. Every night before she went to sleep, she prayed to God for help to be a better wife and mother.

* * * *

Bill really loved it when he was super happy because he felt brilliant and powerful. He loved the attention that salesclerks gave him when he bought expensive presents for Elizabeth and Angela. He hated it when Elizabeth tried to keep him from spending money. He thought she was deliberately trying to make him angry. He constantly reminded her that he was the head of the household and he could spend money on anything he wanted. When he was feeling super happy, it was easier for him to tell her off about anything she did that didn't please him. He grew to love watching her cower when he yelled at her because it made him feel powerful. Sometimes he acted as if he were going to hit her just to watch her shrink away. Still, he loved the way people looked at him when he was out with Elizabeth and Angela. He knew he was the envy of every man they passed, and he fantasized that all women wanted him. He was careful to never show his moods while he was at school. He had perfected 'the perfect teacher' persona and no one at his school ever saw the real him.

CHAPTER 43

In the fall of 1989, he was so deeply depressed that he broke down and cried in front of Elizabeth. "I just want to die. I'm a complete failure as a husband and father. You and Angela deserve better than me. I should just kill myself! You two would be better off without me."

Elizabeth held him in her arms and rocked him to try to calm him down. Hearing him talk like that made her afraid that he would try to kill himself, and he had that damn gun in the top drawer of the dresser. "You're a wonderful husband and father. I know you never thought you would end up being a high school teacher but you're great at it." Bill just said, "I would have been a great lawyer." He was angry at himself for breaking down in front of her because he was usually able to hide his true feelings. He smashed a lamp, but it didn't make him feel any better.

A few months after Bill broke down in front of Elizabeth, he came out of his depression again. He felt okay for a while and then reached the point when he was gloriously happy again. That phase didn't last long and he went back to feeling just okay for a short period of time. It wasn't long before he started sinking into another depression. The time between his depression and being gloriously happy was getting shorter.

Elizabeth still didn't recognize a pattern emerging in his changing moods. Her self-esteem had plummeted to an all-time low because she never stopped blaming herself for his moods. All she could think of was that she had pushed to buy the house and she quit taking the pill, which resulted in a pregnancy that kept him from going to law school. She was getting older and she believed him when he said that she looked frumpy. She focused on the fact that he had gone along with everything she wanted, and those things kept him from fulfilling his dream.

She was grateful that he hadn't hit her recently. She was afraid that she would set him off and he would hit her again. Lately, when he lost control, he smashed something in the house. She had to replace dishes, lamps, vases, and a window, but he didn't hurt her again. She kept a close eye on how he treated Angela but all she saw was a dad who adored his little girl. At least that was one thing she didn't have to worry about. She never told anyone what was going on and she felt more and more isolated.

CHAPTER 44

Elizabeth looked forward to working with her students when Bill was in one of his moods. Helping to develop their talents was almost therapeutic for her. She felt good about being able to help them and teaching art was something she knew she did well. Her principal and other teachers all praised her work saying she had a special way with her students. When she heard about a new art class for public school teachers, she jumped at the chance to get out of the house once a week to learn something new. Because the class was free and she already had the painting supplies, Bill had no objection to her taking the class.

Teachers taking the class were asked to apply for a grant to take a two-week, art course in Paris. The grant would be awarded to forty-eight teachers in the US. It was based on a sample of their painting and an essay they wrote on how they used art to inspire students to continue their education. She wasn't going to apply but her instructor insisted. He said her paintings were some of the best he had seen. The trip was scheduled during summer break when teachers were free to travel. She was excited about the opportunity, but thought that Bill would automatically say no. She timidly brought it up to Bill.

"My instructor says that he'll send in a recommendation for me. I would love to go to Paris to study, but I would hate to leave you and Angela. I doubt that I would win the grant anyway. Hundreds of art teachers will apply. Do you think I should apply?" She was surprised by his answer.

Bill said, "Your work is better than I've seen in galleries and I think you should definitely apply. It sounds like an opportunity of a lifetime. We have to keep Angela in daycare during the summer so that she doesn't lose her spot anyway. I'm perfectly capable of taking care of her when she's at home. I really want you to go for it." He thought she didn't have a chance at winning the grant and there was no harm in letting her apply.

"Okay, I'll apply but I am not getting my hopes up. Out of the hundreds who apply, only forty-eight will be picked. I doubt that I would even be considered but I appreciate your support. Knowing that you are behind me means the world to me. Help me pick out a painting to submit."

Elizabeth spent several evenings writing and rewriting her essay for the grant. Bill helped her pick out the painting she was going to submit. They chose a picture of Elizabeth holding Angela that she had painted when Angela was one. She really didn't think she had a chance at winning, but it was fun to dream.

When Elizabeth received the news that she had indeed won the grant, Bill appeared to be happy for her. Now that she had actually won the grant, she started to worry about leaving Angela for two weeks. He had never been mean to Angela, but she worried that the added stress of caring for Angela by himself might throw him back into one of his moods. She watched him carefully for a few days to see if there was any sign that he wasn't okay with her going to Paris. He continued to act as if he was happy about her winning the grant. Finally, she decided she would go to Paris because an opportunity like this might never come again. When Bill brought home a bottle of champagne to celebrate, she was convinced that he wanted her to go.

* * * *

Bill was thinking, *I can't believe she won the damn grant. I have to act like I'm happy about it. Otherwise, everyone will think I'm a jerk. We've never been apart since we met. How do I know that she won't find someone else on that trip? I still have several months to stop her from going. Maybe I can think of something to stop her that won't make me look like a jerk.* His thoughts kept going back to the fact that she would be with other men while she was away. He knew that she was a desirable woman, but he had always been there to keep men away. He started obsessing about it, but didn't voice his thoughts. He brought home the champagne to keep her thinking that he was happy.

* * * *

His teaching career was going well. Some days when he was really depressed, his history stories sounded more like a lecture that any history teacher would give. When he was normal or 'too happy,' his stories brought history to life for his students. He gave in-class research assignments on days when he was feeling really bad. The students just thought he had to give those assignments to comply with the curriculum, and they always cooperated without complaining because they loved him. The principal and teachers at the school thought the world of him, too. It was rare that a teacher could engage students to the point where they were eager to learn. No one at his school had any idea that he wasn't perfectly fine.

CHAPTER 45

Elizabeth called Donna to tell her about the upcoming trip to Paris. Donna hadn't heard Elizabeth so excited since she called with the news that she was pregnant. She teased Elizabeth about becoming a world traveler.

Donna asked, "How's Angela doing? I can't believe I still haven't seen her. I'll bet she is just gorgeous and really smart." Elizabeth was so proud of Angela that she went into great detail about Angela's life. Donna had never seen Angela, who was now three, because she had taken on the additional responsibility of training new sales representatives. She had been traveling the country and hadn't been home for longer than a week since before Angela was born. She and Ed spent their limited time together at home just being with each other. Donna said she couldn't believe that so much time had passed since they had seen each other.

When Donna asked about Bill, Elizabeth decided to tell her about Bill's depression. She was feeling isolated and needed someone to talk to about him. She knew that Donna would keep her confidence. It didn't occur to her to tell Donna about his spending sprees and she certainly didn't want Donna to know that he was prone to violence.

"Bill goes into deep depressions sometimes. He's upset that he isn't a lawyer and he feels like a failure. He's a great teacher, but that doesn't matter to him. Sometimes I wish that he would smoke pot again. It might help lighten his mood, but he doesn't believe that a teacher should be using pot."

Donna responded, "I know a few teachers who still use pot, but most of them just drink a lot. They all say that teaching is really stressful. There's a new antidepressant on the market and it's different from the older antidepressant drugs. This one affects the level of serotonin, which regulates mood. The great thing about this drug is that it has almost no known side effects. I know several people who are taking it. They call it their 'happy pill'. Bill can easily get a family-practice doctor to prescribe it. It isn't addictive, so doctors don't have a problem writing prescriptions for it. All teachers probably need to be on it. I don't know how teachers put up with the kids today."

Elizabeth said, "Teaching is tough but nothing like what you do for a living. I couldn't handle all that travel and the pressure of having a quota to make. I'll mention the drug to Bill and maybe he'll try it. I really miss talking to you. I knew I could count on you to have an answer. You always do. You also remember things from college that I would rather forget." Elizabeth was laughing as she teased Donna about remembering everything.

Donna said, "I really miss you, too. I wish that I could come to visit but I have to go to Dallas to train some new reps. When I get back, I have two days at home before I have to go to San Francisco for a big surgery convention. It is a tough job but the money is great and Ed is used to being alone. Sometimes, I think if I was at home all the time, we would be divorced by now. When you get back from Paris, I promise I'll figure out a way to see you. Keep sending pictures. At least with the pictures, I know what Angela looks like. If you ever need anything, I'm always here for you."

"I have to run. No telling what Angela has gotten into. I'll talk to you soon and thanks again for helping me." She felt like a weight was lifted from her shoulders when Donna told her about the new medicine, and it felt good just to tell someone a little of what she was experiencing with Bill. Talking to Donna made her realize how isolated she had been feeling. She decided to wait to see if he got depressed again before she brought up the new medicine. She didn't want to have that conversation unless it was necessary. He was still very sensitive about breaking down in front of her and she didn't want to do anything to upset him.

* * * *

Elizabeth had no way of knowing that the real reason Bill refused to use pot again was because it kept him from experiencing euphoric periods that he loved so much. He had smoked a joint with one of his friends when he was in a 'too happy' phase. It had brought his euphoric mood crashing down. After the pot was out of his system, he had regained the euphoric mood. He knew he would never use pot again.

* * * *

If Elizabeth had told Donna about Bill's 'too happy' moods, Donna would never have recommended an anti-depressant. She would have told her that he needed to see a psychiatrist because 'too happy,' plus having depressive episodes, equaled bipolar disorder and those patients needed strong anti-psychotic drugs. She also knew that the drug could make bipolar symptoms worse.

CHAPTER 46

In April, just after Angela's birthday, Elizabeth suspected that Bill was very depressed again. He was coming home from school, eating dinner, and going straight to bed. He didn't spend much time with Angela or her. Anytime she asked him how he was feeling, he said that he must be fighting off a virus or he had a rough day. She didn't buy his excuses because the behavior had been going on for weeks. He looked terrible and she was worried about him.

She made spaghetti for dinner one Wednesday evening when he was depressed. They ate at the kitchen table with Angela sitting in her high chair between them. Angela was eating her spaghetti with her hands and her face was covered with red sauce. Bill usually made slurping noises when Angela ate spaghetti, but he was silent and just picked at his food. Elizabeth decided it was time to talk to him about the pills Donna told her about. She was really stressing out about talking to him because she wasn't sure how he would react, but she couldn't put it off any longer. She chose her words carefully.

"Bill, I know that you've been feeling down lately. There are a bunch of teachers at my school who've started taking a new anti-depressant drug. They call it their 'happy pill'. It has almost no side effects and it really makes them feel good. You might want to try it. It might make you feel better."

"I'm fine. I just need to get more rest."

She plunged forward, "You don't even have to see a shrink. Any doctor can write the prescription. You're a great teacher and you've set the bar really high for yourself. It's no wonder you get depressed sometimes. I'm telling you the teachers are all raving about it. Just for me, please think about trying it."

Bill knew that Elizabeth was pushing really hard. He probably wasn't hiding his depression as well as he thought. "The last couple of months of the school year are really rough. You know the kids can smell freedom and it's hard to keep their attention. Maybe I could use something to help me get through these last few months. I'll try it, but if it makes me feel bad, I won't take it."

"I just want you to be happy."

"I know you do. I'll make an appointment tomorrow. Like you said, it's worth a try."

Elizabeth was relieved that he hadn't gotten angry and hoped that the pills would bring him out of the depression. She cleared the dishes and put Angela to bed. By the time she finished, Bill was already in bed asleep. The conversation had gone well but she was still stressed. She poured a glass of wine and went to sit alone in the living room. As she settled on the couch, she realized that she was really looking forward to her Paris trip. Even though she loved Bill and Angela, she needed a break.

Bill went to see a family practice doctor who had an office close to the school where he was teaching. The doctor was a young, athletic-looking man. Bill instantly liked him and he sensed that the doctor would be sympathetic to an overworked teacher. Bill told the doctor that he was depressed because of all the hassles that came along with teaching high school kids. He asked the doctor to give him a prescription for the drug Elizabeth had told him about.

Bill made a point of not telling the doctor about his childhood illness. His juvenile record was sealed and he didn't want anyone to know about what had happened years ago. That didn't have anything to do with what was happening to him now. No way would he put his job in jeopardy by bringing up ancient history.

The doctor wrote out the prescription without hesitation. He patted Bill on the back and said, "I don't know how teachers do it. It must be so difficult teaching kids who don't want to learn." Bill nodded in agreement and took the prescription. As he left the office, the doctor said, "Make an appointment for six months from now, we'll see how you're doing then."

Elizabeth was standing at the stove and holding a piping hot cup of tea when Bill walked in the back door. She offered the cup to Bill and turned to make a cup for herself. Angela was watching cartoons in the living room. They sat at the kitchen table and sipped the hot tea without speaking. Bill pulled the bottle of pills out of his pocket. "I am going to try these 'happy pills'. If they make me feel bad, they're history." Elizabeth kissed him and told him she was glad that he had gotten the pills. For a few weeks after he started taking them, he did seem to be better. He wasn't sleeping as much and he was actually being nice to her. He seemed more like the Bill she married than the Bill she had been living with for years.

CHAPTER 47

After a few more weeks of taking the pills, he became very irritable again. He stayed in the little office anytime he was home and he rarely played with Angela. He was surly and angry all the time. However, he didn't direct his anger toward Elizabeth or Angela. He was angry about everything else in his life. Elizabeth couldn't think of anything she could do to help him other than let him have his space. It never occurred to her that the pills might be causing this new behavior because Bill being irritable wasn't a new thing. She was just grateful that his anger wasn't directed at her for a change.

School finally ended for the year and Elizabeth's trip was only four weeks away. In the hopes that Bill would feel better once school was over, she hadn't changed her plans to go on the trip. She used the time when Angela was in daycare to clean the house and run errands to get items she needed for her trip.

Bill was spending most of his days away from home because he was barely able to control his temper. He hadn't been able to think of a way to keep her from going on the trip, and he was fixated on her being with other men when he wasn't around. He didn't want to give Elizabeth any reason to run into another man's arms while she was in Paris, and he decided it was best to stay away as much as possible. He told her that he was helping Larry with work on the farm. She thought it was probably good for him to have physical activity after being cooped up in a classroom all the time. She had no reason to question what he was doing all day.

Bill was going to Larry's farm every day but he wasn't helping with the work. Bill would walk to the back of Larry's farm every day and shoot at a silhouette target he had set up. When he wasn't shooting, he sat in the middle of the field and read historical fictions. Larry was busy with the farm and rarely talked to Bill when he was there. When Bill came home in the evenings, he would eat and go to straight to bed. He told her, "Working on the farm is wearing me out. I'm not used to physical labor. I want to help Larry as much as I can before you leave for Paris. I'll stay close to home while you're gone in case Angela needs me."

Elizabeth was leaving for Paris on Sunday morning, the 24th of June. The Saturday before she left, they spent the day at the park with Angela. It was the first time in ages that they had been out as a family just to have fun. Angela had a great time playing with the other children in the park and Bill acted like a doting father and loving husband. They made love that night and Bill was tender with her. Before she fell asleep, Elizabeth said a quick prayer thanking God for all of the good in her life and asked him to protect Bill and Angela while she was gone.

Sunday morning, Bill and Angela drove Elizabeth to the airport. She hugged and kissed them both several times before she went inside the airport. She didn't want to leave them but it was too late to change her mind. When Bill assured her that he and Angela would be just fine. Elizabeth teared up and said, "I'll only be gone for two weeks but it will seem like a year. Now that it's time for me to go, I don't want to." He pretended to pout, "You won't go over there and find another man, will you?" Elizabeth told him that she loved him and only him. She promised to call as soon as she arrived in Paris. He smiled and kissed her again before she went into the airport.

Bill was really angry with himself. *Why did I let her go? She's so beautiful. Men will be all over her. I saw the way men looked at her in the park yesterday.* He forced himself to focus on the drive home but he kept thinking about Elizabeth being with another man. He couldn't stand the thought but he couldn't get rid of it.

When he fed Angela that night, he put a few teaspoons of Benadryl in her milk to make sure that she would go right to sleep.

She went right to sleep and slept through the night, leaving Bill to fume as he paced between the kitchen and living room. His mind was racing with thoughts of Elizabeth being with other men. *I'll never let her go no matter what. She belongs to me and no one else is ever going to have her. I'll kill her before I ever let her go.* He took two pills that evening. *If one is good, two might be better.* He hoped the pills would get rid of the thought of Elizabeth with another man. He looked at the clock. *She should have called by now! What the hell is she doing?!*

CHAPTER 48

When Elizabeth finally arrived at the hotel in Paris, she was exhausted from the flight. Her room was tiny compared to American hotel rooms. The room held a small bed, a night stand, and a dressing table with a mirror. A print of Van Gogh's *Starry Night* was hanging above the bed. The bathroom was so small that she could barely turn around in it. She didn't care about the accommodation because she was excited just to be in Paris. The first thing she did after getting into her room was to put a picture of Angela and Bill on the nightstand next to the bed. She stretched out on the bed while she tried to figure out the time difference between Paris and Louisville, but she was so tired that she couldn't concentrate. She decided to close her eyes for a few minutes before she called home. Elizabeth immediately fell into a deep sleep.

Luckily, when she checked in, she left a wake-up call for six the next morning. The ringing phone woke her from her sleep. She picked up the receiver and listened to what sounded like gibberish, then hung up. She looked around at the unfamiliar surroundings and tried to figure out where she was. She quickly realized that she was in Paris and remembered she hadn't called home the night before. She jerked the phone off the nightstand and dialed her home number. She didn't care what time it was in Louisville. She needed to talk to Bill and check on Angela. It was midnight in Louisville but Bill picked up on the first ring.

Elizabeth started telling him that she had fallen asleep when she got to the hotel. Before she could say a word, he was screaming at her.

"I know what time you got to Paris! You said you would call as soon as you got there. Where the hell have you been?"

"I'm so sorry. I was exhausted. I fell asleep as soon as I got in the room."

He was still screaming, "I bet you just fell asleep! You probably went out and picked up the first guy you saw and screwed him!"

Elizabeth was floored by his rant. She couldn't imagine why he would be accusing her of such a thing. "Calm down, Bill! Stop screaming. You're going to wake up Angela. Is she alright?" She didn't wait for his answer, "I know I should have called. I was trying to figure out the time difference when I fell asleep. I'm so sorry. I swear, I've been in the hotel room all night." She was filled guilt for making him worry.

Bill heard the fear in her voice and realized he sounded like he was out of control. If she hadn't already been with another man, he didn't want to drive her to it while he was out of the picture. He took a deep breath as he said, "You're right, I'm being stupid but I was sick with worry when you didn't call. I didn't mean it when I accused you of being with another man. I know you would never do that. I was going nuts waiting for you to call."

She was relieved that he seemed to calm down so quickly. "The flight took nine hours and then another two to get to the hotel. I was completely exhausted because I couldn't sleep on the plane. Are you okay now? I wish that I had never taken this trip, I would rather be there with you two."

Using his most convincing voice, Bill said that everything was fine now that she had called. "I'm okay. Everything is fine now that I know you're safe. Get ready for your class. I'm sorry for being a jerk. I love you. Angela and I will be fine."

She said, "I love you, too, and I do need to get ready for class now. I'll call you on Wednesday. These phone calls cost a fortune." When she hung up, she was shaking like a leaf. She said a quick prayer, asking God to take care of Bill and Angela. Saying the prayer calmed her down and she felt better.

CHAPTER 49

Elizabeth's class was better than she anticipated. The students in the class had been painting for years and relished the idea of getting better at their craft. After meeting in the lobby of the hotel, a guide put them on a bus to go to the Louvre where they would meet their instructor. The morning class included a private tour of the inner workings of the museum and they were allowed to watch an artist restore an old painting. Then, they walked through one wing of the museum and were given detailed information about the paintings there.

By lunch, everyone in the class was hungry and ready for a break. They went to a bistro where the back room had been reserved for the class. Elizabeth was seated between Maggie from Texas and Luke from New Jersey. The menu for their lunch included samples of wine and cheese from northern France. The main course was a rich Boeuf Bourguignon and their dessert was a sweet pastry that literally melted in Elizabeth's mouth. She wished aloud that the dessert had been bigger. Luke was scraping the last bit of pastry from his plate, and Maggie had just put a large bite in her mouth when Elizabeth made the comment about wanting more dessert. They both laughed and nodded in agreement. She blushed and said she hadn't meant to say that out loud.

At the end of the meal, the instructor addressed the group, "During the rest of this afternoon, you will finish your tour of the Louvre. For the rest of the class, you will be separated into twelve teams of four students each. Each team has been assigned an instructor for the remainder of the class." To divide the group into their teams, the instructor walked behind their chairs, counted to four, and then repeated the process until all teams were chosen. Elizabeth's group included Maggie, Luke, and Jennifer. The instructor said, "During the next two weeks, you will get to know your teammates really well. In addition to painting during the day, every evening your instructor will take you to visit museums and galleries. You won't have any free time until Sunday. This is an ambitious agenda, but we want you to get as much out of this class as possible. If there are no questions, we will go back to the Louvre to continue your tour and meet your team instructors." No one complained about the packed schedule. They were ready to soak up every bit of knowledge they could from the class.

Elizabeth frequently thought about Bill and Angela over the next two days. She worried that taking care of Angela on his own would put too much strain on Bill. She had always been there to handle the feeding, bathing, and caring of Angela. She missed Angela more than she could ever have imagined. Each night before going to sleep, she said a prayer asking God to keep Angela and Bill safe and well.

CHAPTER 50

Bill kept Angela home on the Monday after Elizabeth left. He didn't want to deal with anybody, especially that nosey Mary. He hadn't gone to sleep after Elizabeth called because he was angry and wired. He gave Angela more Benadryl on Monday morning and she slept most of the day. When she woke up that evening, he fed her a peanut butter and jelly sandwich, bathed her, and gave her juice with more Benadryl. She slept through the night while Bill paced the floor.

Bill took Angela to daycare on Tuesday. As usual, he didn't stay to chat with Mary. As he handed Angela over to Mary, she asked him about how Elizabeth was doing in Paris. Bill gave her a flippant answer. "She is doing fine. She's in Paris, for God's sake." He went out of the door as soon as Mary took Angela's hand. He didn't want to explain why Angela hadn't been there the day before.

Mary took Angela's hand and walked away. The quick exchange had left her with a feeling that Bill was on edge. She recognized that he really had problems. She noticed that Angela seemed a little sluggish but had perked up by noon, so Mary decided to let it go.

Bill drove straight home after dropping off Angela. His thoughts were racing while he was driving. *What's Elizabeth doing? Who's she with? Why did that bitch at the daycare center look at me like I'm crazy? Oh, yes, I noticed. Mary is a nosey bitch and always asking questions.* He didn't like anybody knowing his business. As soon as he got home, he got out his gun and began cleaning it. He couldn't take the chance that crud in the barrel would make him miss a shot if he needed to take one. As he cleaned the gun, he fantasized about killing Mary.

I'll follow her and wait until she's alone. Then, I'll blow her head off. No one will ever suspect I did it. Too bad, I want people to know that I'll kill anyone who screws with me.

CHAPTER 51

Elizabeth was having the time of her life in Paris. She was being exposed to concepts that she had only read about and never fully understood. On Tuesday, they learned how color could be used to affect mood and emotion. Each person in her group was asked to paint a canvas using only three colors. When finished, each member of the team would describe the emotion he or she felt when viewing the paintings. Her teammates had created paintings that brought out a feeling of joy or peace. Elizabeth painted a picture using dark colors and dramatic lines. She intended for her picture to bring out a feeling of passion, but her teammates said it evoked a feeling of sorrow. The instructor praised her painting and said it was powerful. She was pleased with his praise but unhappy with her picture. She hadn't intended it to be sorrowful. After looking at it from their perspective, she had to admit that it was.

On Tuesday night, they went to three of the larger galleries in Paris to view paintings by artists from around the globe. She was totally comfortable being with her little group. They shared information about their lives back home, talked about what they were teaching their students, and freely gave critiques on the works of art they were seeing. Elizabeth found herself laughing more than she had in years. When she got back to her little hotel room, Bill and Angel's picture was the first thing she saw. She kissed the picture before she went to sleep every night. She felt a little guilty about having so much fun and wished they had been able to come to Paris with her. She tried to push Bill's rant to the back of her mind so that she could enjoy herself.

She called home on Wednesday evening as promised and Bill sounded okay. "I'm having a great time taking care of Angela. I might keep her home the rest of the week so we can spend more time together."

Elizabeth replied, "I wouldn't recommend doing that because Angela needs a routine. Taking care of an active child all day is a daunting task. It would probably be best to take her to daycare."

Bill easily relented, "I guess you're right. She probably is better off staying in daycare." He asked if she liked the people in her class. He wanted to know if there were any guys in the class but he wasn't going to straight out ask. She told him that the class was broken into small teams. Then, she started telling him all about what she had been doing. He didn't press for more information about the people in her class because he knew he would find out during their next phone call. He couldn't do anything about it if there were men in her class.

Elizabeth said, "I love you and miss you both so much. I wish you and Angela were with me."

"I love you, too, but we need to cut this call short. You be careful and have fun."

* * * *

He didn't want Elizabeth to think that he couldn't handle the kid and that was the reason he said he might keep her home for the rest of the week. Offering to keep her home would make Elizabeth think that he was handling everything well. He gave in quickly when Elizabeth balked at his idea because it was better not to have the kid at home all day anyway. He probably couldn't keep her drugged all the time. That much of the drug might hurt her. He didn't think he was giving her enough to hurt her now. Elizabeth had given it to her the last time she had a cold and it was no big deal.

* * * *

Mary noticed that Angela was acting sluggish for a few hours each morning after Bill dropped her off. Oddly, the child would perk up by noon every day. She decided to mention it to Bill just in case Angela was getting sick. When Bill came in to pick up Angela that afternoon, Mary said, "Angela seems a little sluggish in the mornings. Is she sleeping okay? I'm concerned that she might be getting sick."

Bill's answer satisfied Mary's curiosity. "I've been putting her to bed later than she's used to because we're having so much fun together. I didn't realize that keeping her up late was affecting her. I'll start putting her to bed at her normal time just to make sure she's getting enough sleep."

Mary watched Bill take Angela out to the car. He was asking Angela about her day and Angela was happily telling him all about it. He seemed to really adore Angela and she was always eager to go with him. But still, Mary had that nagging feeling that something wasn't right.

The stupid bitch bought it, Bill thought as he was leaving. *It's none of her business what time I put my own kid to bed. Mary is just hired help and she has no right to question me. I'd love to kill that bitch.* The thought calmed him, but not as much as it had before.

CHAPTER 52

Elizabeth called home around noon Louisville time on Sunday. She couldn't wait to tell Bill how much she was learning and catch up on how things were going with Bill and Angela. Bill listened to Elizabeth's litany of what she had been doing. He really didn't want to hear what a great time she was having in Paris while he was stuck at home with the kid, but he pretended to be interested. While she was telling him about the class, she mentioned a guy named Luke being on her team. Bill felt a wave of jealously sweep through him but he didn't say anything then. Upsetting Elizabeth might make her run into that guy's arms – if she hadn't already.

He calmly asked Elizabeth about the two women in her group. Then he asked about Luke. "What about the guy, Luke? Where's he from? What does he look like? What do you think of him?"

Elizabeth didn't think anything of his questions about Luke. He had asked pretty much the same questions about the women on her team. "Luke is a nice guy who is married with two children. He's a teacher in Cherry Hill, New Jersey and he wants to open a gallery someday."

Bill was livid and his thoughts were racing again. *Why does she know so much about that guy? Is she interested in him? Is he putting the moves on her? Has she slept with him? Why did I let her go to Paris!? I'll kill him if he tries to touch her!!!*

Elizabeth was asking for details of what had been going on at home but Bill knew he was close to losing control. He made up a story about Angela helping him cook. As soon as he finished the story, he said that the call was probably costing a fortune. He let Angela say "Hi" to Elizabeth and then he took the phone back, told her he loved her and encouraged her to have fun. He knew he had to get off the phone before he exploded. It was taking every ounce of self-control he had to not go off on her.

She told Bill that she loved and missed him. She asked him to give Angela a kiss for her and she hung up. She had no clue that he was quickly descending into madness.

CHAPTER 53

Bill waited to hear Elizabeth's phone click off before he slammed the phone receiver. He picked up a glass and smashed it against the wall. The sound of shattering glass brought Angela running back into the kitchen. Bill yelled at her to get out of the kitchen before she cut herself on the broken glass. He told her to go to her bedroom and stay there. Angela began to cry and she ran as fast as she could to her bedroom. She knew that Daddy was really mad. Bill could hear her crying and he knew he shouldn't have yelled at her. He grabbed the bottle of Benadryl and poured some into a glass with a little juice. He went into Angela's bedroom.

Speaking as calmly as he could. He told her that he had accidentally broken a glass. He held her in his lap and stroked her hair as he rocked her. "Everything is okay. Daddy just didn't want you to hurt yourself on the broken glass. I'm sorry I yelled at you. Now, be a good girl and drink your juice." She drank the juice as fast as she could. She wanted to please her daddy. Bill put her under the covers and kissed her on the forehead before he left the room. She fell asleep within a few minutes.

Thank God, the kid finally went to sleep. She's really getting on my nerves. Angela slept in a drugged sleep until about five that evening. When she woke up, Bill fed her and gave her more juice loaded with Benadryl. She was asleep by 6:30. He needed peace and quiet to be able to think straight. His rage had gone. Now, all he felt was total despair. He went to bed, too, because he was suddenly very tired.

It was only seven when he went to bed, but he fell asleep and slept through the night. He dreamed of being with Elizabeth and his dream was vivid. They were back in the old apartment without Angela and were really happy. Elizabeth was more beautiful than ever and seemed to glow. A shadow was lurking behind her in his dream. He knew the shadow was going to hurt her but he was powerless to stop it. When he woke up, he was drenched in sweat and filled with dread. Something bad was going to happen. He was sure of it.

Bill waited until noon Monday to take Angela to daycare. She was really groggy and refusing to eat that morning. He couldn't have the bitch at the daycare thinking something was wrong. By the time he took Angela to the daycare center, she was alert and happy as usual. He told Mary that they had gone to the park to play before coming to the daycare. He went straight to bed when he got home from the daycare. He was tired of thinking, tired of worrying, and tired of Elizabeth not being home. He set the alarm to get up when it was time to go back to get Angela and he slept all day. He dreamed again of the monster trying to get to Elizabeth. When the alarm went off, he was more exhausted than he had been when he lay down that morning. As soon as he got Angela home, he fed her a peanut butter and jelly sandwich with more Benadryl in her juice. He went to bed as soon as she was asleep but not before taking a double dose of his pills as he had been doing for days.

When he awoke Tuesday morning, he felt better. Actually, he decided that he felt great. He must have had a virus, which would explain how he had been feeling. Maybe he had been running a fever, which would account for the vivid dreams. He took Angela to daycare and then went to the gun range. Shooting the gun always made him feel better. Today, it made him feel great! He pictured Mary's face on the target. He shot well that day.

CHAPTER 54

Elizabeth's team was late getting back to the hotel Wednesday evening. She didn't have much time before having to go out on their required nightly excursion but she called home anyway. Bill picked up the phone on the first ring. He had been sitting beside the phone in the living room waiting for her to call. The living room was dark and gloomy because a bad summer storm had come in and rain pelted the windows as he sat there waiting for her call. He really needed to talk to her because he had grown more and more anxious about what she was doing with Luke. His imagination was running wild and he couldn't seem to slow his thoughts.

He was only sleeping a couple of hours a night now. He was still drugging Angela, and had figured out just how much it took to put her out and still get her to fully awake in the morning. He tried to keep his voice under control when he answered the phone.

Bill picked up the phone during the first ring. "Elizabeth?"

"Yes, it's me. How are things going?"

Bill responded, "Everything is fine, but I really miss you. I can't wait until you get home on Sunday."

Elizabeth was just beginning to tell Bill the latest news about what she had been doing when there was a knock at her door. She said, "Hold on a minute. There's someone at my door. Let me see who it is. I'll be right back." She laid the phone on the nightstand. Luke was at the door with Maggie and Jennifer, "Come on. We've got to get going."

She responded, "I'll be right there. Just let me get off the phone."

Bill lost the little bit of control he had and was screaming into the phone when she picked it back up. "So, you need to get off the phone to go be with that guy? What are you going to do? Go to his room and screw him? If I ever meet that guy, I'll kill him!"

Being away from Bill's constant criticism had given her the strength to stand up for herself a little bit. "Bill, what's the matter with you? He was with the other two women from my group. We're supposed to meet our instructor in the lobby. You know I have to go out every night. If you think I am screwing around, you're out of your mind! You're driving me crazy! I'm telling you the truth. I'm not doing anything with anybody. Now, get that through your head! I can't stand it when you act like this and I don't need this right now! Stop accusing me of screwing around!"

Her words hit him like a slap in the face. She had never talked to him like that before. He knew that he had crossed the line and now she was really pissed off.

He began to cry. He said he was sorry and begged her to forgive him. Elizabeth knew that she had to calm him because he sounded so crazy. She softly said, "Bill, you know that I love you and would never do anything to hurt you. I'll be home on Sunday and we can talk about it. I promise that nothing is going on between Luke and me. My team has to go out at night. I told you that. He had both of the other women with him when he knocked on the door. Do you believe me? Are you okay now?"

He regained a little control of himself. Using his calmest voice, he said he was okay and he did believe that nothing was going on with Luke. "I'm sorry. But, with you so far away and I heard that guy say he was waiting on you. It just freaked me out! I know you're not doing anything wrong. I just miss you so much. I couldn't stand it if I lost you to another guy."

"You know that I love you and you're not going to lose me to anybody. I really have to go now. Do you want me to call you back when I get in? I'll be back in four hours from the tour. I need to know that you are alright."

"There's no need for you to call back, I'm fine now. You go on and don't worry. I'll pick you up at eight on Sunday night. I can't wait to see you. Just remember that I love you. Don't worry about me. Everything will be okay when you come home." He hung up.

When Elizabeth hung up, she sat on the edge of the bed and tried to figure out what was going on with him. He had never been jealous before. She knew that he was losing it and she had no clue why. Maybe it was too much of a strain for him to take care of Angela by himself. She promised herself, *I'll never leave her alone with him again. Not that he would ever hurt her. I don't believe he's capable of hurting her but he sounded so crazy on the phone. Why did I ever come to Paris?* She looked at the clock to see if there was time to call him back, but she was already late. As she waited for the elevator, she wondered if Bill had stopped taking his medicine.

Bill though that he really screwed up this time. *How could I have been so stupid and lose control like that? She hates jealously and I've always been able to hide it. What the hell is going on with her anyway? She never talks to me that way. She probably thinks she can leave me now that she has another guy. Well, I'll never let her go. She's mine and no one else will ever have her. I'll kill her if she tries to leave me and I'll kill that bastard, too!* It was the first time that he thought Elizabeth could actually leave him and the thought scared him to death. His thoughts bounced from killing Luke to holding her on their wedding night.

When the phone rang, he thought it was Elizabeth calling back. He picked up the phone and said, "I love you." When he heard the voice on the other end of the line, he realized that it was Mary. *Why is she calling? Has something happened to Angela?* He looked at the clock and saw that it was five-thirty! Hours had passed since he talked to Elizabeth. *How did that happen?* He quickly covered by saying, "Mary,

I'm sorry. I was talking to Elizabeth and the line went dead. I guess the storm knocked it out while we were talking. I was waiting for her to call back and I thought for sure that it was her when I picked up. I didn't realize how late it is. I'm leaving now to come and get Angela."

"I was concerned when you didn't pick up Angela at five and thought something might be wrong. I can stay here until six but then I do have to leave. Do you need to stay there to wait for Elizabeth to call?"

"No, we were done talking when the line went dead, and she has to go out to art galleries every night. She probably already tried to call back and couldn't get through. I doubt that she will try to call back now. I'm leaving right now to come to get Angela."

Bill washed his face and used eye drops to hide his red eyes. He took two more pills. As he drove to the daycare, his thoughts were racing again. *What the hell happened? Did I black out? Why can't I think straight?* He knew he needed to get a grip on himself before Elizabeth got home. By the time he got to the daycare center, he had managed to put on his 'life is great' face. He made a point of being very apologetic. He said he was really sorry to have kept Mary there and he wouldn't let it happen again. He embellished on his previous lie, "Elizabeth sounded so homesick when she called and we were cut off midsentence. She's coming home on Sunday. We'll all be glad when she gets back. We won't keep you any longer and thanks again for staying late." Mary just nodded.

She watched him carefully while he was talking. What he was saying made perfect sense. He appeared to be okay, but she noticed that Angela clung to her when Bill reached for her hand this time. She was glad Elizabeth was coming home on Sunday. Her instinct had been telling her that something wasn't right and now it was screaming.

On the way home, Bill stopped at the drug store to get more pills and another bottle of Benadryl. The pharmacist said it was too early to give him a refill on the pills. Bill quickly came up with a lie,

"My wife's mother had a stroke and she had to go and take care of her. She was so upset when she was packing her suitcase that she must have put my pills in the suitcase or she accidentally threw them away because I can't find them. Her mother has taken a turn for the worse and I have to leave tonight to be with my wife. I don't know how long I'll be gone. Can't you just refill it this one time?"

"Given the circumstances, I'll go ahead and give you a refill. There's some wiggle room in the law regarding refills if the drug isn't a controlled substance. I hope your mother-in-law gets better." Bill thanked him as he paid for the pills and Benadryl. *What an idiot!* He swallowed two more pills.

CHAPTER 55

During the tour on Wednesday evening, Luke could tell that something was bothering Elizabeth. When they got back to the hotel that evening, he asked if the ladies would like to join him for a glass of French wine. Maggie and Jennifer declined, saying they were tired and just wanted to go to bed. Elizabeth decided she could use a drink. "I would love to have some wine."

Luke and Elizabeth said goodnight to Maggie and Jennifer, then they walked into the small dimly-lit bar adjacent to the lobby. Most of the people in the bar were members of their class. Luke and Elizabeth stopped to speak to a few of them before going to a table for two.

After ordering their wine, they chatted about their class for a while. Finally, Luke asked, "Is anything wrong? You seemed to be distracted this evening."

Elizabeth started to say that everything was fine until she looked into Luke's eyes. His concern was genuine and he wasn't just making conversation. "My husband has been accusing me of having an affair over here. He heard you at my door and he went nuts. He thinks that you and I have been fooling around."

Luke was floored. "What! I'm a married man. I would never cheat on my wife!"

"I know that but Bill doesn't know you. Bill has never been a jealous husband and I've never given him any reason to be jealous. I just don't know what's wrong with him but he sounds crazy. He was screaming at me over the phone and I'm really worried about him. He's alone with my little girl and I would never forgive myself if anything happened to her. I was supposed to call him when I got to Paris but I fell asleep. I called as soon as I woke up the next morning but he was accusing me of going out and screwing the first man I met. That's not like him. This trip has been so wonderful and I find myself wanting it to never end. I miss my little girl but I feel like I am free for the first time in years. After the phone call this evening, I realized that I've been walking on egg shells around Bill for a while and I don't really know what's wrong with him." She knew she was giving him too much information but she couldn't stop herself. It was a relief to tell someone her troubles.

Luke was a sympathetic listener. "Everything will probably be fine when you get home. People do funny things when in unfamiliar territory, like suddenly having your wife half way across the world and hearing a guy tell her to hurry up and get off the phone."

Elizabeth appreciated Luke's sensitivity. She suddenly found herself very attracted to him. However, when they finished their glass of wine, she said she needed to call it a night. Luke ordered another glass of wine and watched her until she got on the elevator. She was the first woman he had been attracted to since getting married. She was beautiful, intelligent, funny, and sensitive. Maybe it was a good thing they were going home on Sunday. Staying away from her was growing more difficult each day.

CHAPTER 56

Bill made sure that he delivered and picked up Angela at the proper times on Thursday and Friday. He stayed and chatted with Mary for a few minutes each day in an effort to stop her from realizing that something was wrong. He didn't want her to have anything to tell Elizabeth when she got home. He continued taking two pills twice a day.

Bill didn't give Angela any Benadryl on Saturday. He wanted it to clear out of Angela's system before Elizabeth got home. She would notice if Angela wasn't up to par. The drug was completely out of her system by Saturday afternoon and she was a bundle of energy.

She ran through the house and then jumped on and off the couch which caused Bill to lose what little self-control he had. He grabbed her, slapped her leg, and a big red welt came up on her leg. She screamed when he slapped her. He dragged her by the arm to her bedroom and threw her on the bed. He yelled, "Shut up! You're driving me crazy!" She pulled the covers over her head to hide from him. She didn't make another sound until Bill came to get her for dinner. He dumped a can of spaghetti into a bowl and didn't even heat it up for her. She ate it without saying a word.

Bill saw that she had a dark bruise on her leg where he hit her. He knew he had to keep her from telling anyone that he hit her. His demeanor was threatening when he said, "You were a bad girl today and I had to spank you. You better not tell anyone that you got a spanking. I don't want them to know what a bad girl you are. If you tell anyone, I'll spank you again. Do you understand me?" Angela knew he meant what he said and nodded her head without talking. She was scared of him and wished Mommy would come home soon.

CHAPTER 57

Sunday morning, the members of the class gathered outside of the hotel to be transported to the airport. Elizabeth and her teammates were put in the same van. Maggie joked that they were still stuck with each other. When they reached the airport, Maggie and Jennifer quickly said their goodbyes because their flights were leaving within the hour. Elizabeth and Luke had a couple of hours before their flights left and Luke suggested that they have breakfast before going to their separate concourses. Elizabeth quickly agreed. She found herself unwilling to leave him until the last moment necessary. They chatted about all they had learned from the class over breakfast. When breakfast was finished, they lingered over another cup of coffee. It was finally time to leave. Luke took Elizabeth by the arm and steered her to a quiet corner in the terminal.

He looked into her eyes and held her hands, "I've grown very fond of you. If you ever need anything, you can call me. My number is on the class roster. I hope that everything is alright when you get home. You are one special lady and you deserve to be happy." Tears welled in Elizabeth's eyes, "I care about you, too, and I'll never forget you. You made my trip to Paris more special than I could have ever dreamed."

He hugged her tightly and held her for several minutes before letting go. "Our flights are leaving from different concourses. I have to say 'Goodbye' now, special lady." Elizabeth nodded. She was too choked up to speak.

Luke walked toward his concourse but he turned and waved at her before he disappeared into the crowd. Elizabeth was crying when she bought a stuffed bear with a little beret to give to Angela.

When Elizabeth settled into her seat on the plane, she allowed herself to play the "What if" game. "What if" she and Luke had met before they were married to other people? "What if" she had made love to him while they were in Paris? "What if" her life was totally different? She forced herself to stop thinking about Luke. If she were married to Luke, she wouldn't have her precious Angela. She needed to get back to reality. Scolding herself she thought, *I am a married woman with a child and all the "what ifs" in the world aren't going to change that.*

During the flight, she tried to figure out what was going on with Bill. Now that she was going home, she had to face the reality that something was seriously wrong with him. While she was in Paris, she hadn't allowed herself to really think too deeply about it because she had been so busy and couldn't face the possibility that he was actually insane. She silently prayed. *God, please let Angela be okay. Give me the strength to deal with whatever is wrong with Bill. Amen.*

She tried to think of all possible reasons for his recent behavior and nothing made any sense except that he was losing or had already lost his mind. She desperately needed to know if Angela was safe and she grew more anxious with each passing minute. The combination of worry and sitting on a plane for hours took its toll on her. By the time the plane landed, her muscles ached and she had a splitting headache. She didn't consciously realize that, somewhere over the Atlantic Ocean, she had garnered the strength to leave Bill--if necessary.

CHAPTER 58

Bill and Angela were waiting for her in baggage claim. Angela was dressed in long pants but Elizabeth didn't think anything of it. As she walked toward them, she checked Bill out for any sign that something was wrong. He was smiling and seemed normal enough. She hoped that she had just overreacted to the phone calls. She kissed Bill, took Angela into her arms, and hugged her tightly. She pulled the bear out of her purse and Angela squealed with delight when she saw it. Angela grabbed the bear and pronounced that its name was Bearie.

After Bill retrieved the bags, they headed for the car. Elizabeth put Angela down to walk to the car but she wanted her Mommy to carry her. Although her whole body was aching, she gladly carried her baby to the car. Angela tightly clutched Bearie as Elizabeth put her into the car seat. She smiled at Bill, "I brought you something, too, but it can wait until we get home. I'm so glad to be home. I really missed you two." Bill didn't say anything as he started the car and pulled out of the parking lot. Elizabeth leaned back in her seat for the drive home. She closed her eyes and immediately fell asleep.

Bill was in the middle of a story that he had made up about Angela's latest antics. When she didn't respond, he glanced at her and realized she was asleep. He growled, "Well, I guess I'm boring the shit out of you!" He was practically seeing red as he drove home. He pulled into the driveway and shook her shoulder. She instantly woke up quickly when Bill touched her and was disoriented. She had been dreaming that she was in Paris, walking along Rue de Rivoli, and holding hands with Luke. Her eyes blinked and the world came back into focus. They were home. "I didn't realize I had fallen asleep. I guess I am more tired than I thought. I must have jet lag."

Bill mumbled something she couldn't understand as he got out of the car. He retrieved the luggage while she got Angela out of the car. On the way into the house, she told Bill that all she wanted to do was take a shower and go to bed. He glared at her but she couldn't see his face in the dark.

DESTINY

CHAPTER 59

Bill took Elizabeth's suitcases into the bedroom while she sat on the couch in the living room holding Angela. She was so glad to be home with her little girl. Bill came into the living room, "Would you like some hot tea?"

"I'm going to put Angela to bed and take a shower, but I would love some tea when I get out."

He started to agree but then he remembered the bruise on Angela's leg. "You go ahead and get in the shower. I'll put Angela's pajamas on her and you can kiss her good night when you get out of the shower." She looked around the living room while Angela was going potty and thought. *It's really good to be home.* When Angela came out of the bathroom, Elizabeth went in to take a long hot shower.

Angela was in bed when she got out of the shower and she went in to kiss her good night. She sat on Angela's bed humming a lullaby as she watched Angela fall asleep. Angela grabbed Elizabeth's thumb before she fell asleep. She was holding Elizabeth's thumb so tightly that Elizabeth had to pry off her little fingers. She was so touched by Angela holding her thumb that tears of love welled in her eyes. *Angela hasn't done that since she was a baby.*

Bill was trying his best to act as calmly as he could, but he was seething and his thoughts were flying. *Elizabeth is finally home and all she cares about is Angela. She wasn't even able to stay awake for the ride home. She should have been really excited to see me after being gone so long. If she hadn't been screwing her brains out in Paris, she'd be all over me.*

The hot shower helped Elizabeth's muscles relax and her headache was easing, but she was very tired. Wearing a robe and having a towel wrapped around her head, she went into the kitchen where Bill was waiting with the tea. The hot tea felt good going down her dehydrated throat. It had a funny taste, like cherries, but it wasn't unpleasant. As she sipped the tea, she started to feel even groggier than she had before her shower.

Bill hadn't said anything since she walked into the kitchen. He sounded sincere when he finally said, "You look exhausted. Why don't you go to bed? We can catch up in the morning. There's no sense in forcing yourself to stay awake."

Elizabeth agreed that she could barely keep her eyes open. Maybe getting some sleep would be a good idea. "It will be so great to sleep in my own bed for a change."

She finished her tea and went into the bathroom to dry her hair. She was too tired to style it. She just wanted to get it dry so that she could crawl into her own bed and sleep. She couldn't remember ever being so tired. She went into the kitchen and kissed Bill goodnight. "I'm sorry that I'm such bad company tonight, I promise tomorrow I'll be as good as new." Before she drifted off to sleep, she said a quick prayer thanking God for her family and asked him to keep them safe.

Bill was pacing around the kitchen. He had put Benadryl in Elizabeth's tea. She was tired anyway and he knew the Benadryl would put her right out. He needed time to think without having to listen to the phony details of her trip. *She probably didn't even go to any classes. She probably met that bastard the first day and stayed in bed with him the whole time. She can't hide the truth from me. She's been screwing that guy the whole time. I noticed that she just gave me a quick kiss at the airport and all she cared about was Angela. I was going to make love to her tonight but she was too tired to even fix herself up for me. Now I know the truth! She was screwing that guy the whole time she was gone!*

He needed to plan what to do next, but he was having trouble concentrating. He knew he would never let her go. *If that bastard didn't live in New Jersey--if that's even true--I would go out right now and kill him.* Suddenly, it dawned on him that maybe the whole story about winning a grant had been a ruse. *Maybe the bastard lives here in Louisville and she was seeing him when she was supposed to be taking the art classes. He's probably a rich attorney. That bastard probably paid for the trip. Elizabeth must have laughed her ass off when she got on the plane, but I'm too smart for her. I figured it out!* Finally, around four that morning, he fell asleep on the couch.

Elizabeth woke up when Angela pulled her hair about seven the next morning. She smiled at Angela and gave her a kiss. Angela was holding Bearie and shoved his head onto Elizabeth's face to give a pretend kiss. Elizabeth said good morning to Bearie and then got up, threw on her robe, and went to find Bill. She found him asleep on the couch. Angela ran over and bounced Bearie on Bill's stomach to wake him up. Bill sat up and rubbed his face with his hands while he tried to figure out what was going on. *Elizabeth's home. What time is it? Why am I on the couch?*

He looked terrible. "Did you sleep on the couch all night? I was dead to the world. I don't remember ever being as tired as I was last night."

He tried to remember why he was on the couch. Then he remembered he had drugged her and stayed up most of the night thinking. For some reason, he couldn't remember what he had thought about last night after she went to bed. He needed to come up with an explanation fast. He formulated a lie that would make sense. "You were sleeping so soundly and you were almost crossways in the bed. I didn't want to disturb you because you were exhausted. He remembered the bruise on Angela's leg and knew Elizabeth would ask what happened if she saw it. "I'll get Angela ready for daycare while you make some coffee and fix her breakfast. Then, I'll take her to daycare and we can spend the whole day together." Elizabeth replied that she was looking forward to spending the day with him but he had already taken Angela to her room. While he was with Angela, he reminded her not to tell that he had spanked her and she promised not to tell.

Elizabeth went into the kitchen to start the coffee and get the cereal. When Bill and Angela came into the kitchen for breakfast, Angela was dressed in long pants again. Elizabeth asked, "Isn't it too hot for long pants?" Bill shrugged and said, "That's what she wants to wear". Elizabeth let it go because Angela was at the age where she liked to pick out what she wanted to wear. After breakfast, Bill left to take Angela and Bearie to daycare. Elizabeth got in the shower as soon as they left. She wanted to do her hair and put on some make-up to look pretty for Bill when he got back. She was hoping they could spend the day in bed together.

CHAPTER 60

After she styled her hair and put on makeup, she made Angela's bed and cleaned up her breakfast dishes. She felt like she had a hangover, but chalked it up to jet lag. She was really glad to be home with Angela and Bill. *It'll be good to be home with a normal routine for a few weeks before school begins. Bill seemed okay last night and this morning. Maybe I exaggerated the phone calls in my mind because I felt guilty for having so much fun in Paris.* She poured a cup of coffee and glanced over the newspaper headlines while she waited for Bill to return home.

When Bill took Angela into the daycare center, Mary asked if Elizabeth had made it home safely. Bill flashed his best smile and said, "Yes, she got in about eight last night. She was tired from the trip, so I let her sleep in this morning. She'll be in to see you later. I know she wants to tell you all about her trip. I've got to run. I promised Elizabeth that I would take her out for breakfast this morning."

He left before Mary could say anything else. She noticed that Bill almost ran to his car. She smiled because she thought it wasn't a meal he was excited about getting.

Bill was so angry that he shook violently as he drove home. He was going to confront her because it was high time she realized that he was aware of her being with that Luke bastard. He heard someone whisper, "It's time to put the bitch in her place and show her who's boss." *Who said that?* He looked over his shoulder to see who was in the back seat, but he was alone in the car.

CHAPTER 61

The second Bill stormed through the door, Elizabeth saw the wild look in his eyes and knew that something was horribly wrong. She jumped when the back door banged loudly against the wall. He was screaming obscenities and calling her vile names. He kicked a kitchen chair and sent it flying across the kitchen. She had no idea what had upset him but the look in his eyes really scared her.

"What's wrong!? What happened!?"

Elizabeth backed away from him as he let out his pent-up rage. "You whore! I know that you've been screwing that guy Luke. Do you think I'm stupid? I'll kill him if I ever see him! You had that bitch Mary checking up on me while you were gone. Well, she didn't see anything because I'm not the one who's screwing around!"

Elizabeth knew that he had gone over the edge. He was ranting like a mad man and she didn't know what had set him off. She knew she needed to speak quietly and calmly. Before she could say anything, he grabbed her shoulders and shoved her against the wall. She hit the wall so hard that the breath was knocked out of her. She tried to move away from him, but he grabbed her by the throat and squeezed as hard as he could. His face was red and his eyes were almost bulging out of their sockets. She was terrified. *He is going to kill me!* She was pinned against the wall and couldn't get loose.

He screamed at her, "I'll kill you before I let you go!"

She couldn't breathe. Frantically, she tried to pry his hands from her throat but his grip grew stronger. She was getting light-headed and knew she was going to pass out if he didn't let go. Without thinking about the consequences, she hit him in the face with her fist. When she hit him, her diamond ring sliced through his lower lip and blood spurted out. The punch caused him to loosen his grip slightly. She pried his hands away from her neck and gulped in a breath of air.

She shoved him back with all the strength she had. "Don't you dare touch me again! What the hell is wrong with you?!" She had shoved him back far enough to get away from the wall. She grabbed the kitchen chair, swung it between them, and then held it up in the air so that he couldn't get close to her. She jumped from side to side behind the chair to stop him from grabbing her again.

Instead of coming at her, Bill shoved past her and ran into the bedroom. He jerked the dresser drawer open and pulled out his gun. He intended to kill her. As soon as he looked at the gun, a wave of self-hatred swept over him. He hadn't been man enough to keep her out of another man's arms, and he had screwed up big time when he choked her. She would never forgive him for putting his hands on her again. He wanted to die.

Elizabeth followed him to the bedroom, but she stayed in the doorway in case she needed to run. She saw that he had the gun in his hand and she screamed, "Bill! No!" He knew he needed to get out of there before she took the gun away from him. He leaped forward and grabbed her by the arm. He swung her onto the bed but she hit the corner of it and bounced off of it onto the floor in front of his feet. Terrified, she crawled away from him and expected to hear a gun shot at any moment.

Instead of a gunshot, she heard him raving, "You won't have to worry about me anymore. I won't stand in your way. You can have that bastard after I'm gone!" By the time she staggered to her feet, he had already stormed out of the room and out of the house. He jumped into his truck, gunned the engine, and backed out of the driveway. The tires were screeching and the truck was swerving as he drove away.

Adrenaline coursed through her veins as she ran to the back door to try to stop him. She knew that he meant to kill himself. He was already backing out of the driveway by the time she got out of the house, and he had taken the gun with him.

CHAPTER 62

Oh God! What if he goes after Angela!? Elizabeth's hands shook so intensely that she could barely dial the daycare number. It took several rings before Mary answered. Elizabeth begged God to keep Angela safe as she listened to the phone ringing in her ear.

As soon as Mary answered, Elizabeth screamed into the phone, "Bill has lost his mind! He left here with a gun! I don't know if he is coming after Angela but lock the doors and call the police. I think he's going to kill himself and he might want to take Angela with him!"

Mary had been trained to handle this type of situation and she had a security plan in place. She quickly said, "Elizabeth, get out of there now in case he comes back! I'll make sure Angela is safe. I'll call the police and get them over here. Do as I say and get out of there now! Call me as soon as you're somewhere safe."

Mary hung up and ran to lock the doors. *Damn, I knew something was wrong with him, but this was worse than I ever imagined.* She called out to her assistant, "We have a Code Red!" Code Red meant there was a possibility of gunfire. Mary had trained her assistant to keep the children in the upstairs' hallway during a Code Red so that any bullets coming through the windows would not reach the children. If the house was breached, the assistant was to barricade the children in the master bedroom and keep them in the walk-in closet with that door closed. Mary had the children practice Code Reds and Fire Drills every month. The children didn't realize that this wasn't a drill and they trooped upstairs quickly as they had practiced.

Mary called the police and told the dispatcher the situation. She gave a description of Bill and his truck, plus his license plate number. She kept that information on file, as well as pictures of each person approved to pick up a child from her daycare. She believed in being prepared for anything when it came to protecting the children in her care.

Her next call was to her friend Henry, who was a retired Metro police officer. Henry had promised to be available if a situation like this ever arose. When he answered, Mary said that she had a Code Red. Henry didn't ask for details. He immediately said he would be right there and he hung up. He called his old precinct and asked for additional patrol cars to be sent to the daycare. He told the dispatcher that Metro had already been contacted. They readily agreed to send additional cars to Mary's neighborhood. When it came to protecting children, Metro pulled out all stops. Three patrol cars were already driving through the neighborhood by the time Henry arrived at the daycare center.

Elizabeth could barely stand. She steadied herself by holding onto the kitchen counter. She frantically tried to think of where else Bill might have gone. She remembered that Bill had been spending time at Larry's farm before she went to Paris. She tried to call Larry but the phone rang four times before the answering machine took the call. Everyone at Larry's farm was in the garden. She left a message that Bill might be coming there and he was armed and very dangerous.

She was worried that Bill might show up before Larry got her message, and she called information to get the number of the police department in the town closest to the farm. She told the dispatcher it was an emergency and she needed to talk to the sheriff. The sheriff picked up on the first ring. She told him what happened and why she thought Bill might be going to the farm. The sheriff knew everyone in his small county. He remembered Bill and the trouble Bill caused years before when Bill and his family lived in the county. He assured Elizabeth that he would run over to the farm to check on things. "If he is going to the farm, I'll get there before he does and try to talk him down. You get out of the house right now and go somewhere safe. If you haven't already called the police there, do it now!" Elizabeth was sobbing as she hung up the phone.

CHAPTER 63

She knew that Mary and the sheriff were right. She needed to get out of there in case he changed his mind and came back for her. She ran into the bedroom and grabbed a suitcase that was still packed from her trip. She dumped everything onto the floor and threw the suitcase on the bed. She quickly picked through the clothes on the floor and threw a shirt, jeans, and some underwear into the suitcase. She ran into Angela's room and gathered up some clothes and a few toys. She dragged the suitcase into the kitchen.

Elizabeth pulled her keys out of her purse and ran out to her car. She threw the suitcase in the back seat, jumped into the driver's seat and shoved the key in. When the car started, she put it into reverse and stomped her foot on the gas. She was shaking badly as she sped down the street.

Elizabeth was still trying to think of where Bill could have gone and she was in the grips of hysteria. *I don't know what to do. If he went after Angela, maybe I can stop him. Maybe he went to Larry's. He's going to kill himself. I know it! I need to get to Angela. She's my baby and I have to protect her! If Bill is there, maybe I can stop him from taking her. I've got to calm down! I have to believe everything is going to be okay.* She ignored the speed limit as she raced to the daycare center.

Elizabeth jumped out, ran up to the door, and pounded on it. Henry came to the door with his gun in his hand. Mary had gone upstairs to help with the children but she had already given Henry a picture of Bill and Elizabeth. He checked the picture. Then let Elizabeth inside and locked the door behind her. She ran upstairs and pulled Angela into her arms. She said, "I'm so-o-o sorry! I don't know what's happening to Bill. He was fine when he left to bring Angela here but he was completely insane when he got back to the house. I'm taking Angela to my friend Laura's. I'll call you as soon as I know something." Angela was struggling in Elizabeth's arms. "No mommy, we can't go! Code Red!"

Elizabeth was confused by what Angela was saying, then Mary realized that Angela was trying to tell Elizabeth that they had to stay there until Mary said it was okay to go downstairs. Mary stroked Angela's hair as she said, "It's okay. The Code Red is over. You did real good, honey. It's okay to go with your mommy. I'm so proud of how well you did during the Code Red."

Elizabeth finally understood what Mary was talking about. She spoke quietly to Angela, "Mommy is so proud of you for knowing not to go downstairs during a Code Red. You are my very smart baby. Now that the Code Red is over, we can leave. We're going to Laura's house for a visit." Angela beamed at Mary and Elizabeth because they were proud of her.

Mary gave Elizabeth a quick hug and told her to be safe. When Elizabeth and Angela were out of the building, Mary started calling the other parents. She told them the situation and tried to reassure them that their children were safe. She advised the parents not to come to pick up their children until she called back. Mary knew that some of the parents would come anyway but they wouldn't be able to get to the daycare. Henry had asked Metro to block off the street after Elizabeth arrived. He didn't want other parents in harm's way if Bill did show up.

CHAPTER 64

The sheriff sped over the dirt road leading to Larry's farm with his siren blaring and the lights flashing. He wanted to have time to warn Larry and secure the area before Bill arrived. Dispatch gave the information about Bill's truck to the county officers and state police in the area. Larry was working in the field next to his house when he heard the siren rapidly approaching. He was surprised when the patrol car pulled up in front of his house. Larry ran over to the car as the sheriff got out. The sheriff quickly explained what was going on with Bill. Just as he was finishing the story, his radio crackled to life. An officer had seen Bill turn onto the road to the farm. "Stay with him but don't pull him over. Let him get here. I know him and may be able to talk him down. If he stops or turns around, call me back. Larry, you all get in your house and stay there until I give you an all clear. We don't want anyone to get hurt if we can help it."

Bill saw the police car following him and reached down to pick up the gun. His thoughts were so jumbled that he really didn't know what he was doing. He slowed down but kept driving. He didn't care what was going to happen. He hoped that, with any luck, the cop would shoot him. He didn't believe in God but he knew that religious people believed that committing suicide would damn you to hell. If the cop shot him and there actually was a God, he wouldn't be sent to hell. As he rounded the curve leading to Larry's, he saw the sheriff's car. Then he saw the sheriff standing in the middle of the road with his gun in his hand. He pulled in behind the sheriff's car, rolled down the window, and threw his gun out onto the ground. The sheriff slowly approached the truck in case Bill had another gun in the truck. He kicked the gun out of the way and then ordered Bill to put his hands up where he could see them and to get out of the truck. Bill meekly did as he was told.

The sheriff said, "What's going on, Bill? Your wife called and said that you had a gun and might be thinking of killing yourself."

Bill's thoughts were too jumbled to formulate an answer. He just stood there looking at the ground. The sheriff moved closer and held out some handcuffs. "Bill, I've known you for a long time. I'm not going to hurt you but I need to put these cuffs on you. Just stay calm and turn around."

Bill still didn't speak. He put his hands behind his back and turned around. He felt the cuffs tightening around his wrists and finally spoke, "Why don't you just shoot me and put me out of my misery?"

The sheriff spoke softly to him. "Now, there is no need to do that. Whatever is wrong, we can work it out." He opened the back door of his cruiser and told Bill to get inside. After Bill was safely locked in the car, the sheriff called out, "All clear!"

Larry ran out of the house and asked the sheriff what was going to happen to Bill. He had listened to Elizabeth's message while the drama was unfolding in front of the house. The sheriff said that Bill hadn't broken any laws, but it was obvious that he was in a bad way. Larry positioned himself with his back to the patrol car window so that Bill wouldn't be able to see his words.

"Can you get him to a hospital with a psych ward? He's having another one of his episodes. He hasn't had one in so long that we pretty much thought he got over it. I guess once you're crazy, you're always crazy."

"Yes, given the circumstances, I can get him in for an involuntary seventy-two-hour observation."

"Let's take him to a hospital in Louisville, if that's okay? The county hospital isn't really set up to take care of this and, besides, he needs to be near Elizabeth."

"I think you're right about that. He would be better off in Louisville. He's going to need a doctor there anyway."

"Is it alright if I go with you? Bill needs someone he knows to be with him right now."

"Well, we don't normally allow a civilian to ride in the car, but maybe having you in the car will help keep him calm. You can ride up front with me." The sheriff called his office to tell them he was transporting Bill to a hospital in Louisville. He told the dispatcher to let Metro know that Bill had been apprehended peacefully.

Bill didn't speak a word during the ride to Louisville. He had no idea how he had gotten into the patrol car. The last thing he could remember was taking Angela to daycare.

After receiving the information that Bill was in custody, Metro called off the search for his truck and contacted the daycare center to let Mary know that Bill had been apprehended. She gave Metro Laura's home number so they could get in touch with Elizabeth. She started helping the children get ready to go home. The road was open and parents were already pulling up in front of the daycare center.

CHAPTER 65

Laura answered the phone when Metro called. She handed the phone to Elizabeth and took Angela from Elizabeth's arms. Angela was only a young child, but she was reacting to all of the powerful emotions going on around her. She was screaming that she wanted Mommy to hold her, not Auntie Laura. Laura carried her throughout the apartment and tried to get her to calm down while Elizabeth was on the phone. Angela couldn't be consoled and screamed louder. Her little face turned red as she struggled to get out of Laura's arms. Elizabeth saw Laura struggling to hold onto Angela and she got off the phone as quickly as possible.

When Elizabeth hung up, she took Angela into her arms again. She sat down on the couch with Angela in her lap and began rocking and speaking softly. Angela stopped screaming and began to settle down. Exhaustion from throwing such a fit finally took over her and, secure in her mother's arms, Angela fell asleep. Elizabeth held her for a few more minutes to make sure that she wouldn't wake up, and then she carefully laid Angela on the couch. Laura was in the kitchen putting cookies on a plate to give Angela when she woke up. After she put pillows against Angela to prevent her from rolling off the couch, Elizabeth went into the kitchen.

"They're taking Bill to University Hospital for seventy-two hours of observation. I need to be there to sign some papers and talk to the doctor. Will you be okay with Angela?"

Laura said, "Bill needs serious help. Don't let him get out until they find out exactly what's wrong with him. You can't take a chance that something like this won't happen again. I can see the bruises on your throat. Did he choke you?"

Elizabeth shrugged, "He was out of control and I don't think he even knew what he was doing. I do think he would have killed me if I hadn't hit him. I don't have time to talk about it now. I just hope they can find out what is wrong with him and fix it. I'll be back as soon as I can to get Angela. I put some of her toys in the suitcase so that she has something to play with. Turn on some cartoons when she wakes up and give her the toys. She should be fine as long as you're calm. Thank you for rescuing us. I don't know what I would have done without you."

Laura hugged Elizabeth and said, "Be careful. You're still really freaked out and I don't want you to get into a wreck. Don't worry, Angela and I will be fine. We'll have some cookies and milk when she wakes up." Elizabeth hugged Laura again and then headed for the door. She stopped in the doorway to look back at Angela to make sure she was still asleep. *What in the hell has the poor child been through while I was gone? Why did I ever go to Paris?*

CHAPTER 66

When Elizabeth arrived at the emergency room, the sheriff and Larry were waiting for her. The sheriff said, "Bill has been admitted to the psych ward and they sedated him. He'll be out for a few hours. A Dr. Arnez has been assigned to his case and he wants to see you as soon as you are finished in the Admissions' Office. They told me to tell you to go to the fourth floor nurses' station and a nurse will get the doctor for you. I'm sorry that you're going through this. At least we were able to stop him from hurting himself or anyone else. I have to get back now. You take care of yourself." Elizabeth thanked him for all of his help. Larry asked the sheriff if he could give him a minute to talk to Elizabeth. The sheriff said he would wait in the car while Larry talked to her.

Larry led Elizabeth to two empty chairs in the waiting room and sat down next to her. "Do you know what happened when Bill was a teenager?"

Elizabeth said that Bill told her he accidentally burned down the family house and had been sent to juvenile detention because of it. She had a sinking feeling that the story Bill told her wasn't true. "What really happened back then?"

"I'm so sorry that no one told you. He set the fire deliberately and that wasn't all he did. He tried to throw a pot of boiling water on his mother and he beat his brother so badly that his brother needed surgery for a ruptured spleen. He wouldn't stay on the medicine that the doctors gave him. I think they said he had something called manic depression. His parents couldn't handle him and that's why he was sent to juvenile detention. They forced him to stay on the medicine while he was in there. When he got out of there, he seemed fine."

Elizabeth was shocked. "Why didn't somebody tell me!? I should have known this before I married him! For God's sakes, I was in Paris for two weeks and Angela was alone with him! I never would have left her alone with him if I had known he had a history of mental illness!"

"We kept an eye out for any signs that he was still crazy when he got out of the detention center. But, after time went by and he was fine, we all figured he had outgrown it or the diagnosis was wrong to begin with. I'm so sorry that we didn't tell you. I'll never forgive myself for not talking to you about this before now. He said he would kill me if I told you and I believed him. But, that's no excuse."

"I knew he was depressed sometimes, but then he would be okay for a while. I wish you had told me, but I can understand that you were afraid of him. I'll definitely tell the doctor he was diagnosed with manic depression when he was young. Maybe there's some new medicine that will help him now." They stood up and Larry told Elizabeth to call if she needed anything and then he quickly left. He couldn't stand seeing the pain of his betrayal in her eyes.

When Elizabeth arrived on the fourth floor, she asked the nurse where she could find a doctor named Arnez. The nurse directed her to a small waiting room and said she would have the doctor come in as soon as possible. While Elizabeth waited for the doctor, waves of anger, guilt, and sadness swept through her. She would never forgive herself for leaving Angela with a mad man.

After waiting for what seemed like an eternity, the doctor came in and asked Elizabeth to walk with him to his office down the hall. Dr. Arnez was an older man with kind eyes and white hair. She felt at ease with him as soon as she saw him. When she was seated in his office, he began by explaining that Bill was still sedated and in restraints. "It will take at least twelve hours before the sedative wears off. If he's calm when he wakes up, we'll remove the restraints. We won't be able to have a final diagnosis until we can talk to him. I need you to tell me what's been going on with him and anything you know about his medical history."

She said, "His cousin just told me that he was diagnosed with manic depression when he was a teenager, and he was in juvenile detention for years because he burned down his parents' house. Bill told me about it but he said it was an accident and his parents just wanted to get rid of him. I had no reason not to believe him because he was so normal at the time. I can't believe he lied and no one told me he was sick before I married him. I don't even know what manic depression is. He was fine when we first got married but then he started having bouts of depression. I talked him into taking that new anti-depression drug because everybody said it was great and it had no side effects." Although he didn't interrupt her, he frowned when she mentioned the drug Bill had been taking. Elizabeth continued by recounting the details of their phone conversations while she was in Paris. Then, she told the doctor the graphic details of Bill's attack. She was shaking by the time she finished her story.

Dr. Arnez said, "I appreciate your candor. Everything you told me will be useful in making my diagnosis, but I suspect that he does suffer from manic depression. The disease is now called bipolar disease. I'll get his medical records and see what was going on." He gave Elizabeth a crash course in bipolar disease.

"The standard therapy for bipolar disease is lithium used along with a powerful antipsychotic drug. Bipolar disease usually starts at the onset of puberty, as it did with Bill. The disease can go into remission for years but returns in the patient's 20's or 30's. Bipolar patients suffer from severe depression and also have periods of extreme euphoria. Between the depressive phase and the manic phase, they appear to be perfectly normal. During the depressive phase, the patients sleep more than normal. During the manic phase, they sleep very little. When patients experience mania, they believe they are very creative, brilliant, and invincible. Their thinking is often erratic. Many of them go on spending sprees that put their finances in disarray. They usually have above-average intelligence and are very charming. Often, people don't even realize that anything is wrong with them because they become experts at hiding their symptoms. Bipolar patients refuse medication because they crave the manic phase. They are willing to live with the severe depression that the disease brings because they know it will eventually lead to the manic phase. Left untreated, the depressive state can overlap with the manic state causing a total break with reality, which is what I think happened to Bill today. Another possibility is that he was in a manic phase and then slipped straight into a deep depression without a period of normalcy in between. Rather than exhibiting symptoms of depression, the patient is consumed with rage and acts on that rage. Either way, it's a formula for disaster. The suicide rate is much higher in these patients compared to other mental illnesses. Sadly, when they take their own lives, they often take others with them. You're lucky he didn't kill you this morning."

Tears were flowing down her face as she talked, "Everything you said has been happening for a long time. He would go into depressions and then be okay for a while. He must have been in the manic phase when I thought he was acting 'too happy'. When he became like that, he spent money like it would never run out and he always talked about being brilliant. I never put the two moods together because there was so much time between them. Now that I look back, it does seem that the period of time between the extremes was getting shorter. How could I have been so stupid? What pushed him over the edge? Did the antidepressant drug he was taking make him worse? I practically forced him to take it!"

"Although that's a possibility, we'll never know whether it made a difference or not. If he was taking a recommended dose, it's doubtful that it made a difference. But, if he was taking more than recommended, it could have brought on the psychotic break sooner than it would have naturally occurred. From what you've told me, his disease was progressing anyway. As far as you not making the connection in the moods, he probably worked really hard at hiding his symptoms and you only saw what he couldn't hide."

She hesitated, "One thing I didn't tell you is that over the last several years, he became abusive. He threw fits and smashed dishes, vases, and other things. He hit me a couple of times but he always apologized."

"He was feeling inadequate and needed to tear you down to build himself up. Maybe it's the disease or maybe he's just a bully. You were there and an easy target. Was there anything about his life that consistently made him unhappy?"

"He always wanted to go to law school but we never had the money. I thought it was my fault because I wanted to buy a house and then I got pregnant. I know he blamed me for not being able to go to law school. He teaches high school history and he's a great teacher. The students and staff adore him, but he always focused on not being a lawyer when he was depressed."

"Just so you know, even if he had gone to law school, he would have found something else to focus on that could have been the cause of his depression. He was trying to justify his depression and it was easy to blame someone else for his problems. His depression is caused by a chemical imbalance. Even if he won the lottery, he wouldn't have been able to escape being depressed without proper medication."

"His cousin said that he wouldn't take his medicine when he was young."

"Sadly, that is also typical of the bipolar patient. We give them lithium to elevate their moods and an anti-psychotic to keep them under control. The combination blunts most of their emotions and slows their thought processes somewhat. However, the biggest reason they refuse to take the medicine is because they love the euphoria that the manic phase brings. They describe that feeling as glorious and they'll do anything to be able to experience it. They are very difficult to manage from a medical perspective. If you don't have any other questions, you should go home and get some rest. You've been through a lot today. You can see Bill tomorrow after three, but I want to meet with you again before you see him. I'll be better equipped to give you a definitive diagnosis then." She stood up to leave and said, "Just one more question. Will he still be able to teach?"

Dr. Arnez assured her that, if he took his medication, there would be no reason why he couldn't continue to teach. That was the only good news she had gotten since all of this began. He watched her as she walked away and thought she was a classic example of a battered woman. He made a mental note to give her the name of a counselor who specialized in that area.

When she got to Laura's, she told Laura everything that had happened throughout the years. Laura wanted to tell her to get out of the marriage now, but she knew that Elizabeth had been through too much that day to even consider it. Now was the time to be supportive, so she said, "Now that you know what's wrong, things will be better." Elizabeth said she hoped so.

When Elizabeth and Angela got home, she saw the empty bottle of the antidepressant pills in the trash can in the kitchen. A cold shiver ran through her body because she knew that he shouldn't have been out of the antidepressant until she got back from Paris. Then, when she got Angela undressed to take her bath, she saw the bruise on Angela's leg and asked how she got it. At first, Angela refused to answer her. Elizabeth asked again, "It's okay to tell Mommy what happened. Mommy really wants to know." Angela wouldn't look at her but answered, "I was bad and Daddy spanked me. I promised I wouldn't tell that he spanked me. Daddy said people would find out what a bad girl I am if I told. I'm sorry for being a bad girl." Angela started to cry. Elizabeth hugged her tightly and told her over and over that she wasn't a bad girl. She gave Angela a bath and read her a story after she put Angela and Bearie to bed.

She was angry at herself for ever leaving the defenseless child alone with him and promised she would never leave her alone with him again, even if he was on medicine. Bill hadn't just gone crazy when she got back, he had been crazy the whole time she was gone. She called Mary to tell her what was going on and to ask if she had noticed anything unusual about Bill while she was gone. She was desperate to know how bad it had been while she was gone and she knew she would never get the whole story out of Bill.

Mary chose her words carefully because she didn't want to say that she always thought something wasn't right about him and she didn't want to scare Elizabeth unnecessarily. "He didn't bring Angela in the day after you left but I didn't think anything of it. She did seem a bit sluggish in the mornings but she had always perked up by noon. Last Wednesday, he was late picking her up. He said that you had called and had been disconnected. He said he was late because he was waiting in case you called back." Mary heard Elizabeth gasp. She didn't press the issue, but she knew that Bill had lied about waiting for Elizabeth to call.

"Bill will be in the hospital for a few days until they get him stabilized on medicine. I'm so sorry for all of the trouble that this has caused. I hope you don't lose any clients because of this mess."

One parent had already told Mary she wouldn't bring her child there anymore. She thought Elizabeth didn't need any more on her shoulders, and she made light of the situation. "Most of the parents are grateful that I have these security measures in place. If I lose some clients because of what happened today, I have a waiting list. Don't you worry about that, you have enough to deal with."

"I'll bring Angela over at noon tomorrow, if that's okay. I need to go to the hospital in the afternoon to talk to the doctor and to see Bill."

"That'll be fine. I'll say a prayer for Bill's speedy recovery. Try to get some rest tonight."

Elizabeth had a raging headache and went to the medicine cabinet in the bathroom to get some aspirins. When she opened the cabinet, she saw the empty bottle of Benadryl sitting next to one that was half-full. She instantly knew why Angela had been so groggy in the mornings and then she remembered the cherry taste of the tea Bill gave her. For a moment, she hated him. But, then, she remembered he was sick.

CHAPTER 67

When Elizabeth arrived at the hospital the next afternoon, she asked to speak to Dr. Arnez before she went in to see Bill. She only waited fifteen minutes before he came to see her. "I've started Bill on lithium and an anti-psychotic tranquilizer. I received his medical records from the state and his records substantiate the bipolar diagnosis. Is he a heavy drinker or does he use drugs?"

"Bill drinks wine occasionally, but not every day. He used to smoke a lot of pot, but he stopped that when he started teaching."

"There are some studies being done on the use of marijuana with bipolar patients. Nothing conclusive has been found. However, in some patients, it did appear to help control the symptoms of the disease. His heavy use of marijuana might have masked the symptoms of the disease or he may have been in remission during that time. We'll never know the answer to that. Bill admitted that he doubled the dose of the anti-depressant and that may have made his condition worse. Given his history of hiding the truth about his disease, I'm not surprised a doctor gave him the prescription. If the doctor had known about the previous diagnosis, he never would have given Bill that drug."

Elizabeth felt like she had been punched in the stomach. "It's all my fault! I pushed him into getting the prescription because I thought it would help him. No one told me that he was mentally ill. He lied to me about burning down his parents' house. He lied about everything!"

"None of this is your fault. You were only trying to help him. If Bill stays on the medicine that I've prescribed, he can live a normal life and continue to teach. You will have to be vigilant to make sure he takes his medication. As I told you yesterday, the biggest challenge we face with this disease is that patients won't take the medication. I have the name of a counselor who can help you through this. You should consider seeing him for your own wellbeing." He handed the card to her.

She stared at the card and said nothing for a while. She got up and went to look out of the window and asked, "Is he going to be dangerous? I have a child and I have to think of her first. I love Bill, but, my first priority is protecting my child."

Dr. Arnez said, "If he takes the medicine, he won't be violent. But, as I said, you have to make sure he takes it. We can only keep him here involuntarily until tomorrow afternoon. I want you to help us convince him to stay here until he has stable levels of his meds in his system. I've assigned a therapist to see him three times a day for as long as he's here. If we can convince him to stay for at least a week, I think he'll be able to resume his life. Are you willing to work with me on this?"

Elizabeth sighed and turned to look at the doctor. "I have to try. He's my husband."

Elizabeth left Dr. Arnez's office and stopped at the nurses' station to be taken to Bill's room. The door to the hallway leading to Bill's room was locked and visitors had to be escorted to the patient's room. Bill was sleeping when they entered his room. The nurse told her that he was lightly sedated. However, if Elizabeth woke him up, he would be able to talk to her.

The nurse left her alone with Bill and she watched him sleep as a flood of emotions swept through her. She noticed that the restraints had been removed, which meant that he must be cooperating. When she got control of her emotions, she shook Bill's shoulder and his eyes opened.

He said, "I'm so sorry. I know what I put you through. I'm sick but I'll do anything to get better." Elizabeth replied, "I know you will and we're going to get through this. I know you didn't mean to hurt me or Angela. The doctor says if you agree to say here for a while, he can get you on the right medication and everything will be fine."

Bill blinked. It was taking a while for Elizabeth's words to get through the fog in his brain. "How's Angela", he asked. "I miss my little girl."

She hesitated. It wasn't the time to tell Bill that she knew about the Benadryl or that she knew he had hit Angela. She finally said, "She's fine. Will you agree to stay in the hospital for a while longer? The doctor says it's important to get you stable on your medicine and it will take a while."

"I'll do anything to get my life back. I swear to you that I'll never hurt you again. You believe me! Don't you?"

"Of course, I believe you. Now get some rest and I'll be back to see you tomorrow." She believed that he meant it now but knew his word was only good as long as he was on the medicine.

Bill smiled and fell back into a drug-induced sleep. She watched him sleep for a few minutes and then left to get Angela. She knew that part of her love for and trust in him was gone forever.

CHAPTER 68

Bill stayed in the hospital for an additional ten days and Elizabeth visited him every day. They both met with Dr. Arnez the day he was released. Dr. Arnez explained the medication regimen and stressed that it was important for Bill to adhere to it. "Bill, you came very close to harming yourself and Elizabeth. It's vitally important that you stay on the medicine as I have prescribed. Without it, your symptoms will come back. I'm here for you and you can call me anytime. I've scheduled weekly appointments for you and you must come to them. Are you willing to take the medicine and keep your appointments?"

Bill said, "I've accepted that I have a disease, and I realize how lucky I am that things turned out the way they did. I give you my word that I'll stay on my medicine and keep my appointments. I never want to go through something like that again. Will I be able to go back to teaching?"

"As long as you take your medicine, there is no reason why you can't live a normal life. Elizabeth tells me that you're a great teacher. You stay on your medicine and you can continue to teach." Bill was relieved that he would still be able to teach.

On the way home, Bill mentioned that the medication really muddled his mind but that Dr. Arnez had said that would change after he was on it for a while. Elizabeth was gripping the steering wheel as hard as she could as he talked. Bill talking about the medicine's side effects made her nervous. She decided to see the counselor that Dr. Arnez had recommended. She needed support from someone who was not close to the situation.

When Elizabeth told her parents about her situation, they were worried about her. They gave her as much emotional support as they could but they couldn't forgive Bill for hurting her. Laura tried to be supportive too, but she often voiced her opinion that Elizabeth might want to think about getting a divorce. Elizabeth wouldn't hear of it and said he was sick and she would stand by him just like she would if he had any other disease. The counselor was helping her with her self-esteem issues and she was feeling better about herself. She found a psychologist who specialized in children for Angela. She wanted to make sure that Angela wasn't emotionally scarred by Bill telling her that she was a bad girl.

Bill continued to see Dr. Arnez every week but he always complained that he felt like a zombie. "I rarely laugh and I have no interest in doing everyday things like reading or watching television. I don't play with Angela anymore. But the worse thing is that I have no sex drive at all. I can't stand it."

Dr. Arnez said, "Bill you know that the medicine makes you feel that way. It's not going to get any better but the drug companies are always looking for new drugs. Just be patient, there may be a new drug for your condition sometime in the future. For now, you have to stay on the medicine to prevent another psychotic break. I'm sorry, but you really don't have a choice as to whether or not to take the medicine. Bipolar disease is a life-long illness."

Bill responded, "I know that I don't have a choice. I'll stay on the medicine."

Bill and Elizabeth went back to their teaching jobs when school started in the fall. She always kept Angela with her, even when she made a quick run to buy bread and milk. She wasn't ever going to leave Angela alone with him again even if he was on the medicine.

CHAPTER 69

At the end of September, one of Bill's students stayed in the classroom after the others left. He walked up to Bill and said, "I was told to take your history class. I like history and was looking forward to your famous stories, but all I'm getting is boring lectures. What a joke!" Bill didn't say anything and just stood there watching the kid stomp out of the classroom.

He sat down at his desk and started thinking. *That damn medicine is ruining everything. I should have been pissed off when that kid attacked my teaching but I didn't feel a thing. This is just no way to live. I feel like a God-damn zombie. I can't go through the rest of my life without feeling anything. Hell, I don't even want to have sex with Elizabeth anymore. Eventually, that's going to be a problem because she needs a real man. I see the damn doctor every week and he's not helping me. All he does is push the pills. Maybe if I just cut back on the medicine and take half, I could at least feel something again. If I start to lose it, I can always go back to the regular dose.* He made his decision.

That weekend Elizabeth noticed that Bill was livelier than he had been since he started the medication. She was glad to see that Dr. Arnez had been right about Bill's adjustment to the medication. Although, it had taken longer for Bill to adjust to the medicine than Dr. Arnez predicted. She checked every day to make sure that Bill took his medicine. As far as she could tell, he did.

After a week of only taking half his dosage, Bill didn't feel so 'foggy.' He actually laughed a few times. It felt good to laugh again. His class lectures were better and the students responded to his teaching with renewed enthusiasm. Bill didn't tell Dr. Arnez that he was only taking half the dosage because he knew that he wouldn't approve. He was cutting the tablets in half and flushing the other half down the toilet. If Elizabeth was counting his pills, the right amount would always be in the bottle. He made a point of taking his pills in front of her. She couldn't see that the pills had been cut in half because he kept them hidden in his hand. The longer he only took half the dosage, the more he thought about stopping the medicine completely. He wanted to feel completely normal again.

CHAPTER 70

Bill heard that a big gun show was coming to town the first weekend in October. It was advertised as having a large selection of antique guns. He wanted to see the old guns and told Elizabeth that he was thinking about going to the show.

Her answer was swift and strong, "Bill I really don't want another gun in this house. If that's why you want to go to the gun show, forget it."

He was sincere when he said, "I understand completely. After what happened, I don't want one in the house either, but I would really like to go and just look at the antique guns. Maybe I'll learn something to add in my lectures."

She didn't want him to go to the show, but it was the first time he had shown any interest in doing anything since he was released from the hospital. She relented but asked him again to promise he wouldn't buy a gun. He promised.

Hundreds of vendors filled the Expo Center selling everything from guns to tee shirts. Bill walked past many of the vendors as he headed straight to the antique gun section. He spent a few hours looking at the antique weapons and he bought a couple of books that had great pictures of the old weapons.

As he walked down the aisle to leave, a booth of shotguns caught his eye. One of them was a sawed-off shotgun. Bill had always thought those weapons were illegal. He stopped and asked the vendor about it. The vendor laughed and said it wasn't for sale but that people were always asking him how much to cut off the shotgun barrels to create a broader shot area. The vendor clearly enjoyed sharing his knowledge and he showed Bill how get the correct measurement to saw off the barrel. He told Bill what type of saw worked best to get a clean cut. Bill listened intently and then asked about another shotgun that was for sale.

He couldn't resist. He bought the shotgun and some shells. He filled out the necessary paperwork to register the gun. Kentucky did not run background checks nor was there a waiting period before taking possession of the weapon. He told himself that the only reason he was buying it was because he might want to go deer hunting with Larry in November. He reasoned with himself, *It's not as if I'm going to keep it in the house. I'll probably take it to Larry's and let him keep it.* Bill drove straight to Larry's farm after he left the Expo Center.

When he arrived at Larry's, he showed Larry his new, prized possession. Larry was upset that Bill had another gun, "Bill, after what happened last summer, I don't think you need to have a gun."

"I just want it for hunting deer. In fact, I want you to keep it here. That's why I drove all the way out here."

Larry decided that Bill was sincere, and he put the gun in his rifle cabinet and put the shells in the drawer of the cabinet. He made some iced tea and they took it out on the back deck to drink.

Larry asked, "How are you doing? You look much better than the last time I saw you."

"I'm taking my medicine and I feel fine. I know I have a mental illness that's not going away and I see the doctor every week. I know how close I came to hurting Elizabeth. I'll never let that happen again."

Bill had spoken so openly and sincerely that Larry believed him. After giving it some thought, Larry decided that it would be okay if Bill came to hunt with him in November. He told Bill he was planning to hunt the first Saturday of deer season. "You're welcome to come and I'll build you a deer stand. There are so many deer this year that we really need to thin the herd. By the way, what does Elizabeth think about you hunting deer?"

Bill smiled, "I haven't told her yet but I will when I get home." When Bill left, Larry thought about calling Elizabeth but decided it was better for Bill to tell her about the gun. If Elizabeth was worried about it, she would call him. He didn't like to meddle in other people's business.

Bill carried his books from the gun show into the house and showed them to Elizabeth. "These will be perfect to use when I teach American history." Elizabeth was relieved because she had half-way expected him to come home with a gun. He took his books into the living room where Angela was playing. Bill picked her up and snuggled with her on the couch. He pretended to read her a story as he looked through the books. Angela cuddled close and giggled when he talked like Donald Duck. Elizabeth smiled as she watched them together. *Things are finally back to normal.*

Bill went to Larry's to hunt deer on the first Saturday of the season. Larry asked, "How did Elizabeth take the news that you bought a gun?"

Bill laughed and said, "She was okay with it as long as you keep the gun here and I don't come home with a deer head." He thought, *What Elizabeth doesn't know won't hurt her.*

When a deer came within Bill's range, he took the shot but missed and the deer ran away. He was upset that he had missed the shot and then realized that he had only practiced shooting at stationary targets. Bill was headed to his truck with the shotgun when Larry asked him why he was taking it. Bill told him he needed to clean it and Elizabeth knew he was bringing it home. He hid the shotgun and shells in the garage when he got home.

Around Thanksgiving, Bill completely stopped taking his medication. He decided he liked the way he was feeling and obviously didn't need to take it anymore. He cancelled all his doctor appointments. He resented Dr. Arnez for putting him in a 'chemical straight jacket'. Within a few days, Bill's mood began to darken. By the middle of December, Bill was in a full-blown depression. He told himself that the depression was just an exaggerated response to his system being without medication. He didn't want to go back on the medication and thought he would be fine in a few days. He hid his depression by telling Elizabeth that he was writing a novel and he stayed alone in the study every night until it was time to go to bed.

The last day of school before Christmas break, the kids at school were out of control. All the teachers were at their wits end dealing with the rowdy students and Bill was no different. He was so depressed he couldn't even think straight. His thoughts raced from one thing to another. Behind all the thoughts, *Jingle Bells* repeatedly played in his mind. During his first class, he decided that he couldn't deal with the students. He told his classes that they could sit and talk with each other. But, if they got too loud, he would assign a paper for them to write during the break. His students thought he was really cool for doing that and they behaved.

CHAPTER 71

Bill got home that evening before Elizabeth arrived with Angela. He brought in the mail and lit the Christmas tree because Angela loved seeing the twinkling lights on the tree. He made a cup of tea and sat down at the kitchen table to look through the mail. There were several Christmas cards in the pile and one of them caught his eye. It had a New Jersey postmark. His hands were shaking as he picked it up and looked at the return address. *It's from HIM!* Rage swept through him. Lately, he had been thinking about Elizabeth and that guy, but he hadn't been able to find any proof that she was still involved with him. *Now I have proof!*

Bill tore the envelope open and read what was written on the card. "I hope you have a Merry Christmas and a Happy New Year. I will always remember the time we spent in Paris. Luke." Bill seethed! Now he had proof that she was screwing Luke in Paris. He knew the message was written in a code so that he wouldn't know what it really meant, but he was smarter than they were. He ripped the envelope into pieces but he kept the card to show Elizabeth that he knew what was going on. *She's done making a fool out of me!*

When Elizabeth opened the kitchen door, she knew immediately that something was very wrong with Bill again. He had that same, crazed look in his eyes that he had when he had the psychotic break. She grabbed Angela by the shoulders and told her to run into her bedroom. Angela saw that her daddy was mad and she ran as fast as her little legs would carry her. She shut the door behind her when she got to her bedroom, but she still heard all the yelling in the kitchen.

She decided to sneak out of her room to see what was happening. She crept down the hallway and saw them go into the living room.

Bill held up the card and ranted that now he had proof that Elizabeth had been screwing Luke in Paris. Elizabeth grabbed the card from him and quickly read it. "This doesn't mean anything Bill. I've gotten cards just like this from other people who took the class. What the hell is wrong with you? You aren't taking the medicine anymore, are you? You wouldn't be acting like this if you were still taking your medicine!"

Bill exploded, "I don't need the medicine! I never did! You just want to control me so you could keep me from finding out about how you were whoring around when you were in Paris!"

Elizabeth knew it was only a matter of time until he would attack her again. She needed to get Angela and get out of there. She ran over to the phone to call Laura to tell her she was coming over. Bill followed her and grabbed the phone. He roared, "You're not calling anyone!"

He hit her in the face with the phone receiver and she fell back onto the couch. He ripped the phone cord out of the wall while he screamed, "You're not going to leave this house either!"

Angela was watching from the hallway. She screamed, "Daddy No! Don't hurt Mommy!" Bill threw the phone at Angela, "Shut up and get back in your room!" The phone hit the wall just above her head. Angela ran back to her room and slammed the door. She hid behind the rocking chair because she was really scared.

She was dazed from the punch, but knew she had to get out of there with Angela before he killed them both. She pushed herself off the couch and headbutted Bill in the gut. He fell back onto the floor. She used those few seconds to run to get Angela. She pulled Angela from behind the rocking chair, picked her up, and ran for the kitchen. Her purse was still on the table where she put it when she came in. With her free hand, she grabbed the purse and ran out of the back door. Bill was still on the floor when he screamed for Elizabeth to come back. "Come back here! I'm not done with you! I'll kill you if you leave!"

He got to his feet and ran after them, but she had already slammed the kitchen door behind her. It took him a few seconds to get it open. By the time he got the door open, she was in the car with Angela in her lap. She locked the car door and frantically searched her purse for her keys. Bill was beating on the car window when she finally got the keys into the ignition, started the car, and jerked the gearshift into reverse. She stomped on the gas pedal and flew out of the drive with Angela still in her lap. Bill ran after the car but he wasn't able to keep up with it. He stood on the lawn and screamed obscenities as she drove away. Elizabeth drove for a few blocks until she was sure he hadn't followed her. She pulled to the curb and left the engine running while she put Angela in her car seat.

Once she had Angela in the car seat, she drove to a gas station that had a pay phone out in front. First, she called Laura to tell her that she was on her way to her apartment. Laura wasn't home and she left a message. Her next call was to Dr. Arnez. His answering service took the message that Bill was off his medicine and dangerous. She gave the service Laura's number and asked for the doctor to call her there. Angela was crying when she got back in the car and Elizabeth tried to calm her down by telling her that everything would be okay. Angela blubbered, "Daddy hates us!"

Elizabeth realized that Angela was terrified. She had to calm her down. "Angela, baby, Daddy is sick. He doesn't hate us. We're going to stay with Laura until he gets better."

When they arrived at Laura's apartment, she used the key she kept to Laura's apartment to open the door. She carried Angela to the couch and held her in her lap. She rocked her back and forth and spoke softly as she tried to comfort the terrified child. When the phone rang, she carried Angela with her to answer it. Dr. Arnez was on the line and she told him what had happened.

Dr. Arnez said, "I just checked. Bill cancelled all of his appointments. I began to suspect that he had stopped taking his medicine a couple of weeks ago. He must have been off of it for a while to be this bad. I'll call him and try to convince him to meet me at the hospital. I don't hold out much hope that he will. You need to get somewhere safe and don't go back home for now."

Elizabeth said she would stay at Laura's until she heard from him. She looked through the cabinets to find something for Angela to eat. *Thank goodness Laura keeps peanut butter in her pantry.* She made a sandwich for Angela and turned on the TV so that Angela could watch cartoons.

Dr. Arnez called Bill at home. To his surprise, Bill answered the first ring.

"Bill, this is Dr. Arnez. I am calling to find out why you cancelled your appointments and to ask you to come in now."

"Did Elizabeth call you?"

"Yes, she said that you were out of control and you hit her and then threw a phone at Angela."

"She's just being overly dramatic. We had an argument. I did not hit her or throw a phone at Angela. I caught Elizabeth in a lie and the bitch couldn't handle it. She left in a huff. I'm perfectly fine."

Dr. Arnez didn't believe him, but knew it was useless to try to reason with him. Nevertheless, he tried one more time. "Bill, please come in and we'll talk about what happened."

Bill said, "No, I don't need to come in today. I'll make an appointment for next week."

That was all Dr. Arnez could legally do, so he told Bill to call him anytime if he needed to talk. He called Elizabeth with the bad news. A wave of hopelessness swept over her as she listened to him. She said she'd be at Laura's if he needed to reach her and thanked him for trying to help. She tried to call Laura at work but Laura had already left for the day.

CHAPTER 72

Bill was really angry. *The bitch called my doctor and she had no right to do that. She's covering her ass and trying to take attention away from the fact that I now have proof she's been screwing around.* A wave of exhaustion hit him and he went to bed. He would deal with her tomorrow.

When Laura pulled into the parking lot, she saw Elizabeth's car and thought, *This can't be good. Elizabeth would've called my office to tell me she was coming over if everything was okay.* The door to her apartment was locked and she was certain now that Elizabeth was in trouble. Laura let herself in and found Elizabeth sitting on the couch with Angela. Elizabeth shook her head to let Laura know that things were bad and not to say anything in front of Angela. Laura tried to sound cheerful when she suggested that they watch a video tape of *Mary Poppins*. Angela perked up and started to sing one of the songs from the movie. Laura put in the tape and they watched the first few minutes of the movie to be sure that Angela was going to be okay if they left the room. Once Angela became engrossed in the movie, they told her that they were going to the kitchen to make some hot chocolate.

While Laura made the hot chocolate, Elizabeth told her what happened. Laura made an ice pack for Elizabeth to put on her jaw where a large bruise had started to form. The events of the evening finally caught up with her and she started to cry. Laura took the hot chocolate to Angela and sat with her for a few minutes. She wanted to give Elizabeth some time to get herself together.

When Laura went back into the kitchen, she told Elizabeth that she couldn't go home, and Elizabeth agreed. They got a few quilts from the closet to make a bed on the floor for Angela. "If he hasn't shown up here by now, he's not coming tonight. God only knows what he's doing. You need to stop hoping that he'll be okay and go ahead and get a divorce. Even if you get him back on the medicine, he'll just go off of it again."

"I know you're right. The straw that broke the camel's back was when he threw the phone at Angela."

Laura opened a bottle of wine. They drank it and then they drank another one. It was midnight when they finally went to bed. Angela had fallen asleep watching *Mary Poppins*. Elizabeth slept on the floor with her and held her close during the night.

When Bill opened his eyes the next day and looked at the clock, it was noon. He rolled over and looked at Elizabeth's side of the bed. It was empty. The reality of what had happened the night before came crashing down on him. He remembered the Christmas card from Luke. *That bitch! She's been whoring around the whole time.* When he walked down the hall to go to the bathroom, he saw the hole in the wall and the phone on the floor. He vaguely remembered that he threw the phone at Angela. He went into the kitchen and made a pot of coffee. He needed to jump start his brain because he was having trouble thinking about what to do next. After he drank a couple cups of coffee, he called Laura's apartment. Elizabeth answered and he tried to get her to come home. "If you come home now, I'll forgive you for whoring around and we can get on with our lives."

She said, "Bill, I know that you're off your medicine. You could've killed Angela when you threw the phone at her. You need to get yourself to the doctor and go back on the medicine now! Stay away from us until you are back on the medicine. I mean it!" She slammed the phone down.

The phone rang again but she let the answering machine take the message. It rang three more times and she let the answering machine get those calls, too. Laura said, "Let's get out of here in case he comes over. Let's go to the mall. We can eat lunch there and pick up a few Christmas presents for my Mom and Dad." By the time they got dressed and ready to leave, it was one o'clock. At the mall, Elizabeth bought pajamas for Angela and a flannel nightgown for herself. She also bought a change of clothes for both of them because she didn't know how long it would be before she was able to go home.

It took Bill a few seconds to fully realize that she had hung up on him. He called back, but the answering machine picked up the call. He left a message filled with obscenities. He called back three more times before deciding that she wasn't going to answer again. He drank the rest of the coffee, dressed, and headed to Laura's with the intention of forcing Elizabeth to come home. It was about one-thirty when he arrived at Laura's apartment. He pounded on the door but no one answered. He kicked the door so hard that he punched a hole in the wood before he stormed out of the building.

He needed something to do to calm down, so went to the gun range. He hadn't been there in a long time. When he walked in, he went straight to the gun counter. He bought a 9mm Glock, two extra clips, and a box of bullets. As required, he filled out the necessary paperwork. Bill stayed at the range for most of the afternoon and practiced target shooting with his new gun. It was a powerful gun and he needed to get used to the recoil. He used all the bullets that he had purchased. By the last bullet, he had gotten pretty good at shooting the gun but he still hadn't been able to quite master the recoil to hit the target as well as he would have liked. On his way out of the range, he bought a few more boxes of bullets and another clip.

He stopped at a hardware store and bought a saw like the one the gun show vendor had shown him. When he got home, he retrieved the shotgun from the garage. He sawed off the shotgun the way he had learned from the vendor. He had missed the deer because it was moving and shortening the barrel would limit the range of the shot, but it would also create a wider pellet pattern which would make it easier to hit a moving target. He wasn't thinking about killing a deer as he sawed off the shotgun. He went to bed after he finished with the shotgun because he was tired and needed to sleep before he dealt with Elizabeth.

CHAPTER 73

Laura was the first one to see the hole in her door when they returned from shopping. After getting Angela settled in front of the TV, Elizabeth listened to Bill's ranting messages. She replayed them for Laura. "You're not going back to that house. You need to get an Order of Protection against him. He's really dangerous."

"If he won't go back to see Dr. Arnez, I'll get one. Maybe he has calmed down enough for me to talk him into seeing the doctor."

She called home. He answered the phone after three rings. It was obvious that he had been asleep. When he first began to talk, she thought he was going to be reasonable.

"I guess you saw the hole in the door. Tell Laura I'll get it fixed. Are you coming home?"

"No, I'm not coming back until you're back on your medicine. I will not take the chance of you hurting Angela. Are you going to see Dr. Arnez?"

"No, I'm not going to see him. I'm perfectly fine. You're the one who has problems. Stay wherever you want. I'll find you! You and Angela belong to me and no one is going to change that. Not you, not Luke, not anyone--you understand me!? You'll come to your senses soon enough and get your ass back here!"

Elizabeth didn't answer him and slammed the phone down. She knew she couldn't reason with him.

Laura said, "He's going to kill you and Angela if you're not careful. He's a raving maniac!"

Elizabeth sat down at the table and thought for a few minutes before she answered, "Unless he gets on his medicine, he will probably try. I'm more afraid for Angela than for myself. He's insanely jealous when it comes to me but he has never said anything about Angela before this. I'm afraid he will try to grab her to make me come back. I'm going to go see his doctor on Monday to find out what we can do about him. I have no idea when he stopped his medicine. But, for him to be this bad, he must have stopped it a while ago. I need to call Larry to let him know that Bill is crazy again."

When Elizabeth called Larry and filled him in on what was happening, Larry had more bad news. "Look, you're going to think that I am the stupidest person on earth. Bill brought a shotgun here back in October. He said he told you about it. He seemed so sane that I invited him to go deer hunting with me. He was fine when he came out here to hunt. I should've called you when he first showed up here with the gun, but he seemed like he was okay. All I can say is, I'm sorry."

Elizabeth was livid and thought that Larry was an idiot. "Larry, I can't believe you didn't call me and tell me he had another gun! You know he's crazy! I can't talk to you anymore right now! Just watch out for yourself." She slammed the phone down and Laura made the comment that Bill's whole family was crazy.

Bill's rage was building, but he decided to let Elizabeth stew for the weekend. He went to the gun range again. He was getting better at handling the recoil of his new gun. He even practiced shooting with his left hand to be sure that he could hit the target no matter what hand he used. He thought she would get tired of living in Laura's cramped apartment and come home with her tail tucked between her legs. All he had to do was wait her out. He thought about Dr. Arnez and knew he would never see him again. Never!

CHAPTER 74

On Monday afternoon, Elizabeth dropped Angela off at daycare and went to see Dr. Arnez. He saw her as soon as she arrived. He questioned her about Bill's behavior in the recent months. After he listened to Elizabeth's description of Bill's behavior over the last few months, he was convinced that Bill had stopped taking his medicine sometime in October.

"It's unlikely that Bill will come back in of his own free will. His behavior in the last few months has been indicative of a person in a depressive phase, but the recent violent behavior points more to a manic phase. Or, he could be in a severe depression that is manifesting as rage. I just don't know without seeing him. Nevertheless, the period of normalcy is obviously missing and that means that Bill's mood swings are close to overlapping. I'm very worried that if the moods do overlap, he will suffer a complete break with reality similar to what happened last summer. As you already know, if that happens, he would be capable of harming himself and anyone around him. It sounds like he is still somewhat rational at this point, but that could change at any time. Elizabeth, you're the focus of his delusion and that means that you're in serious danger. Bill may become suicidal again and decide to take you and Angela with him. Laura is in danger, too, because she's protecting you. He'll view her as a threat. Do you have anywhere the three of you can go that he doesn't know about if you need to get away?"

"I have my parents and some friends that I can go to for help, but I don't want to put anyone else in danger."

"You need to get an Order of Protection sworn out against him. Sadly, if he does have a psychotic break and comes after you, having an Order of Protection won't be any help. However, if you have one in place and he breaks the order, you can have him arrested. Once he's been arrested, we can get him back into the hospital by using another involuntary commitment. You have been lucky so far that he hasn't done any real harm. But, if he has a psychotic break, he's capable of anything. Please do whatever you can to stay safe."

Elizabeth thanked him for his advice and left. Dr. Arnez knew that Elizabeth's situation was going to go from bad to worse and quickly if Bill didn't go back on his medicine.

She told Laura the gist of what the doctor said when she got back to the apartment. Laura shook her head and said, "You need to listen to the doctor and get that Order of Protection. I think that's your only hope of getting him back on the medicine and you need to divorce him."

Elizabeth called Bill to tell him that she'd talked to Dr. Arnez. Bill answered the phone and tried to con Elizabeth into coming home. "Come home, please. I love you. I won't hurt you. I promise."

"Bill, I won't come home unless you check yourself into a hospital. That is final, do you understand me?"

"I don't need to go to the hospital. I've already started taking my medicine again. Come home."

"Stop lying! If you're taking your medicine, why didn't you go to the doctor?"

He exploded, "You are a whore and a bitch! Bring my daughter back now!" She hung up the phone.

Elizabeth and Laura rode together to the daycare center to get Angela. On the drive to the daycare center, Elizabeth told Laura about her will, bank accounts, safety deposit box, and her life insurance policies.

Laura said, "Why are you telling me this now? We're going to get you out of this mess."

"I want you to know this stuff in case something does happen. If anything happens to me, I want you to promise me that you'll take care of Angela. I don't want Angela to ever have to live with Bill if I'm not around."

"Of course, I'll take care of Angela, but now is not the time to talk about that. You and Angela are going to be fine. We'll get Bill the help he needs, eventually." Laura didn't believe that Bill could ever be trusted to take his medicine again. She just hoped that, if he did go back on it, he would stay on it long enough for Elizabeth to divorce him.

At the daycare, Elizabeth filled out paper work that would allow Mary to prevent Bill from picking up Angela. Mary said, "Elizabeth, I'll have to let him take her if he comes to get her. He's still her legal guardian and father. You need an Order of Protection that prevents him from taking her and I suggest you get one as soon as possible."

"I'm going to get one and I'll bring you a copy. Laura is the only other person that I want to be allowed to pick up Angela. He might try to send someone else to get her." As Elizabeth and Laura drove away from the daycare, she saw Bill's truck parked down the block but he didn't follow the car. "Laura, I saw Bill's truck sitting down the block from the daycare center. He's not following us but knowing that he was watching the daycare really scares me. It's Christmas Eve and I won't be able to get an Order of Protection until Wednesday. We're going to have to be really careful until I get one. I think we should stay at my Mom and Dad's tonight." Laura agreed.

CHAPTER 75

They stopped by Laura's apartment to get their clothes and then drove to Elizabeth's parents' house. The house smelled of fresh pine from the Christmas tree when they walked in. Her mother had prepared a big Christmas Eve dinner with all of her favorite dishes. Angela was allowed to sit at the table with the grownups. She ate her turkey with a fork and everyone praised her for being such a big girl. Elizabeth mixed some peas in Angela's mashed potatoes and Angela giggled because she thought the peas looked funny in the mashed potatoes. Elizabeth promised Angela that she could eat some gingerbread cookies after dinner if she ate everything on her plate. After Angela cleaned her plate and ate four cookies. Laura put on a tape of *Cinderella* for Angela to watch while they cleared the table and washed the dishes. No one spoke of Elizabeth's predicament that evening because bringing it up would spoil Christmas for everyone. Nevertheless, it was on everyone's mind.

Once Angela was in bed asleep, Elizabeth's father brought out a tricycle to put together for her to find on Christmas morning. Elizabeth's mother put more toys under the tree while Elizabeth filled Angela's stocking with candy. They played Santa while they listened to Christmas carols playing on the radio.

Elizabeth sat on the couch and looked at the Christmas tree. It was decorated with ornaments from her childhood. Seeing the tree brought back pleasant memories of past Christmases. *If it weren't for the situation with Bill, this would have been a perfect Christmas. I hope that Angela can have a lifetime of great Christmas memories like I do. Bill won't be part of those memories and that's sad, but it's his fault. He made the choice to stop taking the medicine.* She felt safe and at peace for the first time in a long time, but she was sad that Bill had chosen to ruin everything. When it was time for bed, she crawled into bed with Angela. She needed to be near her precious baby.

Before going to bed, Elizabeth's father went outside to check for Bill's truck. He was relieved when he didn't see it. Bill was parked down the street around the corner. Even though he was cold and hungry, he stayed there until about two that morning in case she left.

At two, Bill decided that Elizabeth wasn't going to leave her parents' house that night. He went home and went to bed. He didn't like being alone on Christmas Eve, but that didn't bother him as much as wondering if she had called Luke from her parents' house. He couldn't sleep so he got up at four-thirty. He paced around the house until six when he decided it was time to go and watch her parents' house again.

He had already put his sawed-off shotgun in the truck, but he decided that he might need the Glock as well. He put the Glock under the seat of the truck and the extra clips on the passenger seat. When he got to her parents' house, he pulled into the same spot where he had been the night before. It was Christmas morning and he wasn't worried about someone reporting him sitting in his truck because the streets were deserted. He waited and watched until about ten that morning. It was so cold that his breath was steaming up the windows on his truck. He needed to go to the bathroom and he was getting very restless just sitting in the truck. A light snow began to fall and his view was obstructed even more. He decided to go home.

No lights were on in the house when he returned from her parents' house. The gloominess of the house bothered him. He turned on every light in the house and lit the Christmas tree, but the lights didn't make him feel any better. He built a fire and used one of Elizabeth's paintings as kindling. Then, he turned on the TV just to have a sound other than his own breathing in the house.

Bill sat on the couch and looked at the lights twinkling on the tree. Angela should be at home with him playing with her toys. *I'll be damned if I let Elizabeth take my baby away from me. I'll kill her if she tries.* His thoughts whirled around so fast that he was having trouble remembering what he had been thinking about a few seconds before. *Something about Elizabeth. No, it was something about Angela. Maybe I can think better if I get some sleep.* He left all the lights on and went to bed.

He slept until about five that evening. He microwaved a frozen turkey dinner for dinner but he didn't eat it all because it tasted like cardboard. All he could think about was that he should have been eating a big Christmas dinner with Elizabeth and Angela. It wasn't fair that he was being punished when everything was her fault for having an affair. Bill left his half-eaten dinner, got back in his truck, and drove past her parents' house. However, Laura's car wasn't there. He drove past Laura's apartment where he saw both of their cars. He pulled over and parked on the street next to the parking lot. He stayed there and watched their cars until about nine that night. Finally, he was satisfied that she wasn't going anywhere else that night and he went home.

He had left all the lights on in the house when he went to spy on Elizabeth. When he walked into the kitchen, he saw his half-eaten dinner on the kitchen table. He picked it up and threw it against the wall. *Damn that bitch to hell!* He finally went to bed at about one o'clock and slept for three hours. He dreamed of Elizabeth being taken away by that same dark monster from the dream he had when she was in Paris. When he woke up at five, he was exhausted. He felt like he had been running all night. He brewed a pot of coffee and hoped that it would make him feel better. After drinking the whole pot, he showered and dressed. He drove to Laura's apartment and waited for Elizabeth to come out.

He didn't have to wait long. She came out about 7:30 with Angela. He let her pull out and watched as she drove off before he pulled out into traffic behind her. There weren't many cars on the road so he slowed down to allow several cars to come between their vehicles. With each turn, he was more and more certain that she was taking Angela to daycare. He was going to get Angela after Elizabeth dropped her off. *That cow Mary won't stop me from taking her. Angela is my child and I want her with me. If Elizabeth doesn't like it, she can come home.* He waited down the block for Elizabeth to come out of the daycare. As he waited, he wondered if Elizabeth was going to run to her lover after she dropped off Angela. At some point, while he thought about Elizabeth being with Luke, he decided that the New Jersey postmark on the Christmas card was phony and Luke really lived in Louisville. He could get Angela anytime, but catching Elizabeth with her lover would be so wonderful! He could kill them both at the same time. When Elizabeth came out of the daycare, he followed her instead of getting Angela.

He followed her to Jefferson Street and knew she was going to the courthouse. He parked the truck down the block and walked to the courthouse. He stood in the door of the courthouse and watched her climb the stairs to the second floor. He waited until she was at the top before he climbed the stairs, too. When he reached the top of the stairs, he caught a glimpse of her going into an office. The instant Bill saw the words over the door he knew she was getting an Order of Protection against him. He could barely control himself, but he knew he needed to leave before she came out of the room. He ran down the stairs and back to his truck.

He drove like a wild man on the way home. He ran three red lights and almost hit another car. When he got home, he sat on the couch and waited for the cops to come and serve him. He wanted to see what the bitch had told the judge. She had really crossed the line this time. She was going to pay with her life for betraying him.

CHAPTER 76

Bill saw the patrol car pull into the drive, but he waited until the cop rang the doorbell before he opened the front door. The officer explained that he was there to serve an Order of Protection. Bill took the paper and glanced over it. Elizabeth had testified that he had hit her and thrown a phone at their child. The order barred him from coming within 100 feet of her or Angela. It also barred him from taking custody of Angela at the daycare. He asked for specific details on what he could and could not do because he wanted to be sure that he understood what she had done to him. The officer explained that as long as he stayed at least 100 feet from Elizabeth and Angela, he would be in compliance with the order. He said that Bill could speak to Elizabeth on the phone. However, if he threatened her, he would be in violation of the order. Bill listened carefully, but he was already trying to plan what he would do next. Then, the officer told him he had twenty-four hours to vacate the premises so that Elizabeth and Angela could come back to live there. He hadn't thought of that. *Where will I go? That bitch! How dare she throw me out of my own house!* Bill politely thanked the officer and said he would follow the instructions in the order.

Bill took the papers into the kitchen, sat down, and carefully read every word. He reread the papers to be sure that he understood exactly what she had done to him. He laughed out loud when he finished reading them. There was nothing in the papers that kept him from following her as long as he stayed 100 feet away. *This paper doesn't mean shit! I'll kill her for this! She's as good as dead!* He picked up the phone and called Laura's apartment. When Elizabeth answered, he tried to sound civil to throw her off her guard.

"I was just served papers and I know you are really upset. I'll move out tomorrow afternoon. Angela needs to be in her own house. I promise I won't bother you and I promise to see the doctor. I'm already taking the medicine again. I'll do whatever it takes to make all of this up to you. I just want you back. Do you believe me?"

Elizabeth hesitated for a few seconds. No, she wasn't going to be fooled by this act anymore. "Bill, if you are back on your medicine, that's great. I want you to know that I love you, but I've decided that I want a divorce. I can't live in fear that you'll go off your medicine at any given moment. You're right that Angela needs stability. For God's sakes, don't you realize that she is now afraid of you now? You could have killed her when you threw that phone at her. Find yourself a place to live. You need to be out of the house by three tomorrow. I'll have the police with me when I get there, so you better not be there. Do you understand?"

Bill shook. He was so angry that he could barely speak. He took a breath and said, "I'll prove to you that I'll be okay but I understand that, for now, you want me gone. I'll find an apartment tomorrow morning."

She let out a sigh and said, "You better be gone when I get there. I'll have the police with me." She hung up the phone before he could say anything else. Talking to him was emotionally exhausting for her.

When he heard her hang up, Bill grabbed a butcher knife from the kitchen drawer. He wanted to destroy her and anything that she loved. He slashed one of Elizabeth's paintings and then he went into the bedroom and violently slashed her side of the bed. He took the knife and drove over to Laura's apartment. By the time he got there, he had calmed down enough to realize that he couldn't get to Elizabeth while she was in the apartment. He decided not to waste the trip, so he slashed Laura's tires. He thought it would be too obvious that he was the one responsible if he slashed Elizabeth's tires. He hated

Laura, and making her pay for new tires would be a good way to irritate her.

He had no intention of leaving his own house. He was paying for it and, by damned, he was going to live in it. On the way home from Laura's, he came up with a plan. If Elizabeth had the neighbors watching him, he would make sure they got a show. When he got home, he parked the truck on the street in front of the house so that the neighbors wouldn't miss anything when he left the next day.

Bill sat and fumed in the living room. *She said she wants a divorce. Why is she doing this to me? She wants me out of the way so that she can be with that asshole! That's why! I'll never let that happen! I'll kill her before I let her go!* He forced himself to focus on his plan instead of thinking about killing her. In case the neighbors were watching and reporting to Elizabeth, he was going to carry a suitcase to the truck the next day. Then he was going to drive around until he was sure that Elizabeth and Angela were at home alone. He would go back and teach her a lesson she would never live to remember.

He wanted to be sure that the cops were gone when he came back to the house. If Elizabeth was coming back by three, the cops would be long gone by four-thirty. He decided to park on the block behind their house so that he could sneak back without being seen. It wouldn't matter if she had the locks changed, because he was going to get in through a window. He unlocked the windows at the back of the house. *The stupid bitch won't think about the windows. God, I'm brilliant!*

The next morning, Bill packed some clothes in a suitcase. He threw some clothes around the bedroom to make it look like he had gone through his clothes to choose what to take with him. *I'm too smart for her. If she thinks she can get away with throwing me out of my own house, she can think again! She's going to regret ever screwing with me.* He wrote a letter to Elizabeth and told her that he was sorry and would cooperate with her wishes. He didn't realize that the handwriting looked as if a mad man had written it. It was scrawled all over the sheet of paper. Some of the writing was in block letters, some written in cursive, and many words were misspelled. In his mind, it looked perfectly normal.

He put the dirty dishes in the dishwasher and turned it on. He straightened the living room. Bill went through the house and turned off the lights, but he left the tree lights on. *Nice touch. God, I'm so brilliant! When the cops get here, the place will be clean, and they'll think she's crazy.* At noon the next day, he carried out the suitcase and put it in the truck. He even went back in and carried out an empty box to make it appear that he was actually moving. He locked the front door, got into his truck, and drove away. He could kill a few hours at the gun range while he waited for them to come home.

CHAPTER 77

Laura left the apartment around ten in the morning to buy groceries. When she backed out, she felt the tires thump. She got out and saw that her tires had been slashed. Now she would have to buy new tires and she would have to call a tow truck. She checked Elizabeth's tires and they were fine. She cursed under her breath. *Damn, that bastard doesn't need to remind me that he's crazy. I already know that. I wish Elizabeth had never met him.*

When she got back into the apartment, she told Elizabeth to get Angela ready because they had to go out to buy new tires. Without even asking, Elizabeth knew that Bill had slashed Laura's tires. She found Angela's coat and put it on her. She hoped that she had enough money left on her credit card to pay for Laura's new tires. It was the last week of the month and she had spent almost all her extra money on Christmas presents.

After they bought the new tires, they stopped by a local restaurant for lunch. Laura ordered two glasses of wine and a glass of chocolate milk. She laughed and said they would be "drinking their lunch" that day. Elizabeth tried to force a smile but couldn't. Then, they ordered two large Cobb salads and chicken fingers for Angela.

While they drank their wine, they talked about what to do next. Elizabeth said, "You don't have to go home with us. I'm going to have the police go in and search the house before we even go in. I don't think Bill will be there or try anything because, if he gets arrested, he could get fired. He may be crazy but he's not dumb."

"Okay. I have to stay at home and wait for AAA to come tow my car so I can get the tires put on anyway. You need to get your locks changed."

"I already called but they can't get there until tomorrow morning. I'll keep the doors locked and put some chairs against the doors in case he tries to get in. I'm going to keep my keys at the top of my purse if I need to get out of there fast."

"I'll come over and stay with you after I get my tires put on. I don't like the idea of you and Angela being there alone." Elizabeth said that wouldn't be necessary. Angela wanted her mommy's attention and she interrupted the conversation every few minutes. Elizabeth's nerves were on edge. Using her "You'd better stop now" voice, she told Angela to be quiet and eat her lunch. Angela shrank back in her chair, picked up a piece of chicken, and didn't say anything else. Elizabeth felt awful that she had scolded the child, but she needed to be able to talk to Laura without being constantly interrupted. Any other time, Angela's constant interruptions didn't bother her, but her nerves were frayed. Given the circumstances, she knew that Angela was being as good as any child could be. She promised herself she would be more patient with Angela because none of this was her fault. She ordered a sundae for Angela and told her she was a good girl.

When they got back to Laura's, Elizabeth began packing their belongings to take home, but she decided to leave the pajamas and nightgown there just in case they had to come back. She also left a few of the toys that Angela had received for Christmas. Elizabeth waited until two thirtyquarter to three to call the Metro to get an officer to meet her at her house. When she was ready to leave, she hugged Laura and promised to call as soon as she was safe at home.

CHAPTER 78

The patrol car was waiting outside Elizabeth's house when she arrived. She thanked the officer for helping and unlocked the front door. He went in and searched the house while Angela and Elizabeth waited on the front porch. The officer came out and said, "He's not here. It looks like he slashed up the bed and the bedroom is a mess. I think he has a lot of rage. You need to be careful." He helped her carry the Christmas presents from the car into the living room. As soon as she entered the living room, she noticed that two paintings were missing from the living room. Before the officer left, he handed Elizabeth a card with the address of a women's shelter.

"This is the address for a nearby women's shelter. If he comes back, you should go there. They can protect you. Your family and friends aren't set up to keep him away. I'm sorry that you're going through this at Christmas. If he does bother you, call Metro." Elizabeth thanked the officer and put the card in her pants' pocket.

She called Laura to let her know that she was in the house and safe. Laura must have been outside with AAA because she didn't answer, so Elizabeth left a message. She checked to make sure that the back door was locked, and she saw the letter that Bill had left lying on the kitchen table. Her hands trembled when she picked it up and her blood ran cold as she read it. The letter was a terrifying rant but it was the bizarre handwriting that scared her more than anything. He was clearly in a psychotic state. She pushed a kitchen chair against the back door. She carried another one into the living room and pushed it against the front door. She found the slashed painting on the floor in the hallway. She looked around for the other one but couldn't find it. She went into the bedroom to see the damage Bill had caused. She knew she would have to buy a new mattress, but that would have to wait. After she paid for Laura's tires, she was broke. She remembered her secret stash of money in the closet. She got the money out of her sewing basket and put the bills and some of the change in her pants' pocket.

Angela played with her new toys in the living room while Elizabeth straightened up the bedroom. When she went in to check on Angela, she found her playing Tea Party with Bearie. Elizabeth decided to take down the Christmas tree so that she would be in the same room with Angela while she played. After she saw the letter, she wasn't sure that Bill wouldn't show up and she wanted to be close enough to grab Angela and get out.

She was standing on a chair, taking down the ornaments that were on the top of the tree when she heard Angela squeal, "Daddy!" Elizabeth whirled around and almost fell off of the chair. Bill was standing in the middle of the living room and smiling a maniacal smile. Angela ran to Elizabeth and held onto her leg for dear life. Even the child could see that he wasn't normal. Elizabeth jumped off of the chair and shoved Angela behind her. She saw that Bill was holding her car keys.

"What are you doing here? What do you want? Don't come near us!"

Bill went over and calmly sat down on the couch. He laid her keys on the coffee table. He was still smiling when he said, "You didn't really think you could throw me out of my own house, did you? I told you that I want us to be together again. You might as well face the facts. You are my wife and I won't let you go. Not now! Not ever! You're never going to be with Luke or any other man. I'll raise Angela by myself if I have to."

Elizabeth was terrified when he reached behind his back and pulled out a gun. He laid it on the couch cushion next to him. She edged her way to the middle of the living room and pulled Angela along behind her with each step. She knew she had to get out of there before he decided to kill her. She glanced out of the window and didn't see Bill's truck in the driveway. *Good, his truck isn't blocking my car. If I can get to the keys, maybe we can make it to the car before he shoots me. I just have to keep him talking and try to distract him.* Bill just sat there with that crazed smile on his face and waited for her to say something. She took another step closer to the coffee table and was close enough to grab the keys. If she got the chance.

"Bill now is not the time to talk about this, not in front of Angela. We can discuss it later. Right now, for Angela's sake, I want you to leave. Please leave for a little while until I get Angela in bed. I know we'll be able to work things out. I promise I want to more than you know. But, if you care at all about us, you'll leave now."

Bill shook his head, "No! This is my house, my family, and I'm not leaving! I want to talk now! Sit down!"

She hoped to distract him and asked, "Are you hungry?" It worked. His thoughts were so jumbled that it took him a few seconds to process what she had said. She grabbed the keys, grabbed Angela, and ran for the front door. She shoved the chair and was able to unlock the door and open it by the time he reacted. She grabbed a vase from a small table next to the door and threw it at him. He had to dodge the flying vase. She lunged through the door and slammed it shut. Almost dragging Angela, she ran for the car. She jerked the door open, picked up Angela, and threw her in the car. She shoved Angela into the passenger seat and jammed the keys into the ignition. Angela was crying loudly because she was terrified. Angela had been holding Bearie when Bill came in and she kept Bearie clutched in her hands when they ran out of the house. She was glad she had Bearie with her. She didn't want Daddy to hurt him. Elizabeth turned the key and the engine started. She saw Bill running toward the car, but he didn't have the gun in his hand. *Thank God. He must have forgotten it.* With the car door still open, she slammed the car into reverse. She used her free hand to blow the horn. She kept her hand on the horn in the hopes of getting the attention of some of her neighbors.

An outside light turned on across the street. She threw the car into drive, drove across the lawn, and almost hit Bill. He jumped back and cursed loudly at her. Their neighbor came out and saw what was happening. He ran into his house and called the police. Elizabeth passed a police car flying down her street but she didn't stop. She needed to get as far away as possible.

She pulled into a convenience store, jumped out of the car, and ran to the pay phone. She called Laura. "Get out of the apartment! Bill's probably going to come there. I'm taking Angela to a woman's shelter. You can meet us there. Get out now!" She read the address to Laura and hung up.

When the police car pulled into the driveway, Bill was sitting quietly on the couch. He had hidden the gun under the couch cushion. He allowed the officer to come up on the porch and ring the doorbell before he got up. The officer told Bill that he was there to investigate a domestic disturbance. Bill said he had argued with his wife but that she left. He said she had gone to her friend's apartment to cool off. *God, I can fool anybody, especially these idiot cops.* The officer asked if he could come in and look around the house. Bill said, "Of course, I have nothing to hide." After the officer looked in all of the rooms, he left because he didn't know about the Order of Protection. *I won that round!*

Bill thought they had gone to Laura's and he drove there. By the time he arrived in Laura's parking lot, she had already left. He drove to her parents' house, but neither Laura's nor Elizabeth's car was there. He had no idea where they had gone, but he was damn sure going to find out.

CHAPTER 79

Elizabeth carried Angela to the door of the shelter and rang the bell. Roxanne was working the desk that night. She looked through the peep-hole and saw the terror in Elizabeth's eyes. Quickly, she quickly unlocked the door, brought them in, and locked the door behind them. She ushered Elizabeth and Angela into a small room that had a couch and a few toys scattered on the floor. Roxanne spent a few minutes showing Angela the toys before she sat down to talk to Elizabeth, but Angela just sat there and tightly clutched Bearie. Elizabeth told Roxanne what was happening and that her friend Laura was coming there, too. Roxanne assured her that they would be safe in the shelter and she left to get papers for Elizabeth to sign. When she came back, she had Laura with her.

Elizabeth had been trying to stay composed. However, when she saw Laura, she broke down and sobbed. "I don't even have my purse. He left me a note that terrified me--not because of what it said, but how he wrote it. There's no doubt that he's completely psychotic. What am I going to do?"

Laura sat next to Elizabeth with her arms wrapped around her until she was able to gain some control. Roxanne brought some cans of soda for Laura and Elizabeth, and a carton of chocolate milk for Angela. Angela took the milk and drank it without saying a word. She was scared and her mommy was crying again. She was glad she had Bearie with her. Roxanne gave them a pamphlet about the shelter to read. Elizabeth filled out the papers and then picked up Angela and held her in her lap to try to comfort her. She saw that

Angela had Bearie and was glad the child had something familiar with her.

Roxanne took them to a small room with twin beds and a dresser. A small table with a Bible on top sat between the two beds. "You're lucky we have a room. We're always packed to the rafters around Christmas and New Year."

Elizabeth was surprised by that comment, "I always thought of Christmas as a time of peace. I guess I was wrong."

"The holidays bring added financial stress and much more drinking. Unfortunately, men take out their frustrations on their wives and children."

"How many are here now?"

"We have eight other families right now and we are expecting more to come. Sometimes we have so many that they have to sleep on cots, but we don't turn anyone away. We have a dining room downstairs that doubles as a sleeping room, if we need it. By the way, breakfast starts at seven in the morning. It's just cold cereal and juice, but it's nutritious. The bathroom is down the hall. It has shower stalls and you have some soap and shampoo in the dresser. Towels are on a shelf next to the shower stalls. The pamphlet I gave you gives you the information that you'll need about our rules and the facility. If you need anything else, just let me know and I'll see if I can help. You all try to get some rest now. You're safe here." She left them to go and wait for the doorbell to ring again.

Laura had a small suitcase packed with two nightgowns and Angela's pajamas that she kept at her apartment. Elizabeth helped Angela change into the pajamas and took her to the bathroom. When they got back from the bathroom, she put Angela in one of the beds and crawled in beside her. She held Angela tightly and hummed to her until she fell asleep. Even though it was still early in the evening, Laura had already gotten in the other bed. She turned off the light and told Elizabeth to get some rest. "We'll decide what to do tomorrow. You can't go back home. He's never going to leave that house."

Elizabeth whispered back, "We can't go to my Mom and Dad's. I won't put them in danger, too. I feel bad enough that I brought you into this mess. At least we made it out alive. I should never have gone back there. He's beyond reasonable thinking. I didn't know how bad he was until I saw the letter. I should've left as soon as I saw it but I was stupid. I did remember my secret stash of money that I kept hidden in the closet. I put it in my pants' pocket before he came in. It's not much, but it may be enough for you to buy us some things we need tomorrow. I've been so stupid about all of this, but I never had to deal with anything like this before. I should have left Bill when he was on the medicine and we wouldn't be in this situation. I really thought he would stay on it."

Laura got out of bed, went over to Elizabeth, and stroked her hair. "It's okay. You got out and you're safe. That's all that matters. Stop beating yourself up for doing what anybody would do. I didn't even think he was that crazy. We'll figure out what to do tomorrow. Try to relax and get some sleep."

The next morning, they dressed and went to breakfast. The room was filled with women and children. They all had one thing in common--they looked terrified. Elizabeth's heart went out to them because she knew firsthand the terror they were all feeling. She made a promise to herself that she would do something to help these poor women and children when her own nightmare was over. Elizabeth went to the office to call her parents to let them know what was going on. Elizabeth got down on the floor to help the children draw pictures. Laura smiled. *Elizabeth was born to teach.*

Laura found Roxanne in the office and asked her if she could do anything to help. Roxanne said she appreciated the offer and gave Laura a stack of papers that needed to be put into individual folders. While Laura filed the papers, she asked Roxanne how she had come to work there. Roxanne said, "When I was little, my father was abusive and my mother had to get us out of there. We didn't have anywhere to go and ended up in a shelter. My mother and father eventually got a divorce and my mother and I moved away, but I always remembered how safe I felt that first night at the shelter. When I grew up, I got a degree in social work and came to work here. I guess it's my way of giving back. People just don't realize how many women and children live in abusive situations."

Laura said, "I have to confess. I never really thought about it before. I would like to know more about it."

Roxanne responded, "One in four women experiences domestic violence in her lifetime. Over a million women are assaulted every year and it's usually by someone they know. The laws are terribly inadequate and still favor the abuser. We fight every day to have them changed, but it never seems to be a priority when the legislature is in session. People tend to blame the woman for staying in an abusive relationship. We know that, when they have been abused for so long, they don't have enough self-esteem left to stand up for themselves. The other misconception is that only poor, uneducated women are abused. That's not true. Women who come here are from all walks of life, and some have high levels of education and good jobs. They keep the abuse a secret because they are ashamed and blame themselves. In many cases, they make excuses for their abusers when the abuse comes to light. I'm sorry. I didn't mean to get on my soapbox. But, during this time of year, it's really bad and I get angry."

Laura said, "I don't blame you for being angry. I had no idea that domestic violence is so common." The conversation with Roxanne made her realize why Elizabeth had always defended Bill. She fit Roxanne's description of a battered woman to a tee.

Roxanne changed the subject, "Elizabeth probably doesn't realize it, but when she helps the children draw, it's actually therapeutic for them. Just to have someone pay attention without criticizing means the world to these kids. They come here after experiencing unimaginable horrors, and anything that brings a semblance of normalcy helps them cope." Laura knew that what Roxanne said was true because she had seen how positively the children responded to Elizabeth. "I think it helps her, too. With all of this chaos, working with the children takes her mind off of her plight." Roxanne nodded her agreement.

Laura called her friend, Carolyn, and made arrangements for them to stay at her house until they could find a permanent place for Elizabeth and Angela. Carolyn had a big basement they could stay in until this nightmare was over and she was glad to help. When they left the shelter, Elizabeth promised to come back to continue working with the children. Roxanne thanked her for everything she had already done and said that she was welcome to help anytime.

CHAPTER 80

The basement in Carolyn's house was being used as a recreation room, and it had a small bathroom with a shower. The room was big enough so that Angela would have a little bit of room to play and it had a TV for them to watch. Carolyn moved the couch and TV against the wall, while Elizabeth and Laura carried a mattress down the stairs. Elizabeth and Angela were going to share the mattress on the floor. Angela had a nightmare while at the shelter and Elizabeth wanted to be close to her so that she could comfort her and make her feel safe during the night. With all of the upheaval in their lives, Angela needed constant reassurance that everything was going to be okay. Carolyn commented that the poor child was holding up better than anyone could have expected. Laura whispered that Angela was scared to death and rightly so.

Laura went to the drug store and bought some shampoo, deodorant, toothbrushes, toothpaste, and a few other things that they were going to need. Carolyn said she loved to cook and would provide their meals. Elizabeth's parents brought over some of the toys that they kept at their house for Angela. They wanted the girls to come to their house, but Elizabeth insisted that she wasn't going to put them in danger.

CHAPTER 81

Bill drove to Laura's apartment several times a day. He thought he could catch her and force her to tell him where Elizabeth had gone. As far as he knew, she hadn't been to her apartment since Elizabeth left him. He drove by Elizabeth's parents' house every day but he didn't see their cars there either. Also, he watched the daycare center every morning and afternoon and hoped to catch Elizabeth there, but she wasn't bringing Angela to the daycare either. *Where are they? Probably with that guy! This has gone too far! She's done making a fool of me! She's going to be sorry she did this to me!*

Over the next few days, Bill became more deeply depressed than he had ever been in his life. He couldn't get his thoughts to stop racing enough to go to sleep. When exhaustion forced him to sleep, he had vivid nightmares that woke him. After days of not sleeping and not finding Elizabeth, he became suicidal. For the second time in his life, he wondered if there really was a God and if killing himself would damn him to hell. He chided himself for even entertaining the notion that God existed. He held steadfastly to his belief that there was no after life and this life was all there is.

He sat in the dark living room in the middle of the night and put the gun to his head. He wanted out of his miserable life. For some reason, he couldn't pull the trigger. He waited a while longer and put the gun to his head again. He sat with the gun pointed at his head for a few minutes, then laid it on the coffee table. *Why didn't I pull the trigger?* As he sat and stared at the gun, a thought flashed through his mind. *You don't want to go without them.* He grasped onto that thought. *If I'm dead, Elizabeth will just go be with Luke. Luke will raise*

Angela and she will forget all about me. There's no way I'm going to let that happen! We are a family and we're going to stay a family--even in death! He was more determined than ever to find Elizabeth.

CHAPTER 82

Elizabeth returned to the shelter every day that week to help the children with art projects. Each day, there were new children who had arrived with their mothers. When Roxanne thanked her for coming back, she promised to keep coming. She knew that drawing and painting helped the children forget the nightmare they were living, if only for a short while.

Laura called her boss to let him know that she would not be at work next Monday. He was very understanding and told Laura that he wouldn't dock her pay for the days she missed. Word had spread around Laura's office about what was happening to Elizabeth, and everyone offered to help. Laura's friend, Billie, started a prayer chain to ask God to protect Elizabeth and Angela. Laura and Elizabeth were grateful to all of them and were awed by the many offers of help.

Elizabeth prayed every day. She thanked God for giving her such wonderful people in her life. She prayed that Bill would go back on his medicine and she prayed for God's guidance. She was always much calmer after she prayed because she knew that God was listening. She always believed that, if her prayers weren't answered, God knew what was best for her.

CHAPTER 83

Donna hadn't talked to Elizabeth in a few months. She was finally working at home for a while before going back on the road. On Saturday afternoon, she decided to call Elizabeth to catch up. Bill answered the phone.

"Hey Bill, how are you?"

"I'm fine. Elizabeth isn't here."

"I haven't talked to Elizabeth in so long. I miss her. How's Angela? How was your Christmas?"

"Angela had a great Christmas. Santa was very good to her this year. I'll tell Elizabeth to call you."

"That would be great. I'm finally home for a while and maybe I can come over to see you guys."

"Gotta run, but thanks for calling."

He hung up. Although Donna had acted like she didn't know anything, Bill was sure that Elizabeth had already told her everything. *Screw her! I'll just play along.* He called Laura's apartment and left a message. "Elizabeth, Donna called. She wants you to call her back. I know you told that bitch everything. Her stupid act didn't fool me. Where the hell are you?"

On Saturday, Laura borrowed Carolyn's car to go home to get some clothes for work. They didn't know if Bill was watching Laura's apartment. They thought he might not notice Laura if she was driving a different car. She covered her head with one of Carolyn's scarves and hid her face as she walked from the car into the apartment building. While she was there, she listened to the messages on her answering machine. When she got back to Carolyn's, she gave Elizabeth the message that Donna had called.

Laura met her cousin at the mall that afternoon and they bought some clothes for Elizabeth and Angela. Her cousin bought perfume for Elizabeth and a coloring book and crayons for Angela as a surprise. She hoped that getting a little something extra might cheer them up. She gave Laura five-hundred dollars to use as a down payment on an apartment for Elizabeth and Angela. Laura hugged her cousin and said she was lucky to have such a great cousin. Her cousin said, "If I were in Elizabeth's situation, I would want someone to help me. Tell Elizabeth the money is a gift. I want to help in any way I can. I just wish I could have her live with me for a while, but as you know, I am moving in a few weeks." Laura hugged her again and promised to give Elizabeth the message.

CHAPTER 84

That evening, Donna was pouring wine and Ed was building a fire when their phone rang. Donna answered it.

"Hello."

"Donna, it's Elizabeth. I'm so glad to hear your voice."

"What's wrong? You don't sound good."

"Bill left a message for me to call you. I need to tell you what's been going on. He thinks that I already told you."

"Oh, God it's bad! Isn't it?" Donna didn't know what Elizabeth was going to say but she had never heard Elizabeth sound so upset. She thought something was wrong with Angela and she braced herself to hear the worst. Donna's words got Ed's attention and he stopped what he was doing.

Elizabeth told Donna everything that had happened with Bill. She said Luke's innocent Christmas card had sent Bill over the edge.

"He's bipolar and completely psychotic now. I can't believe that he let me know that you called. He always liked you and maybe that's why he did it."

Donna was shocked and immediately offered to help. "Please come to Lexington and stay with me. You and Angela will be safe here. Ed has enough guns in this house to hold off an army and he knows how to use them. He'll protect you."

"No, Bill might follow me or he might find out I went there. I won't put you all in danger. I've already put enough people in danger. We lived in a shelter for a while and now we're hiding at Carolyn's house. She is one of Laura's friends. We're living in her basement. I know he's trying to find us but he doesn't know about Carolyn. Besides, school starts on Monday and I have to teach. He won't stay on the medicine even if we get him back on it. I'm going to divorce him but I know that he'll never let me go. Right now, I just need to keep Angela safe and away from him."

"Elizabeth, please come here."

"He wants to kill me and he'll kill anyone who is around me. I've sworn out an Order of Protection, but that won't help if he gets to me. He's not supposed to be living in the house, but he won't leave. I don't think I'm going to get out of this alive but I have to do whatever it takes to protect Angela. I've made my choices in life and I've made peace with all of this. If God wants to bring me home, I'm ready. I just pray that God will let Angela live so that she can grow up and have a full life. She is so sweet and innocent."

Donna was crying. "Elizabeth, I love you. If you decide that you can get over here without him finding out, or, if you will let me come and get you and Angela, we will protect you. I promise."

"You've always been my best friend and I love you, too. But I have to deal with him here. I'll call you as soon as I find a permanent place for us to live. Thank you for always being there for me. You were right about him when you warned me that what happened when he was young might be a serious, mental illness. I wish I had listened to you back then. But, if I had, I wouldn't have my precious Angela now."

"Promise me. If you need anything, you'll call. I'll be right there."

"I know you would help me if I asked. As I said, I have to stay here and see it through."

"I'll say a prayer for you."

"Thank you. I love you. I have to go now." She was crying when she hung up.

Ed stood in front of the fireplace and listened to Donna's side of the conversation. He watched as she bowed her head and silently prayed. Tears streamed down her face when she looked up at him and told him everything that Elizabeth had said. Sadly, Ed shook his head.

"You need to prepare yourself for the worst. He probably will kill her if he's psychotic. She's welcome to come here. But, if he means to kill her, he will--no matter where she goes." Donna knew that Ed was right and she said another prayer.

CHAPTER 85

On Monday morning, Elizabeth took Angela to daycare. She kept watching for Bill's truck, but she didn't see it. She ran as she carried Angela into the daycare, in case Bill was already there and hiding. Mary said she would keep the doors locked. If Bill showed up, she would call the police. Elizabeth drove to school, but watched to see if he was following her. She didn't see his truck and prayed that he had come to his senses and gone back on the medicine. *Dear God, please let this nightmare be over. Protect my baby and please make Bill stop all of this and get back on his medicine.* When Elizabeth got to school, she looked around for Bill's truck but it wasn't there either. She wondered if he had gone to school, but she knew better than to call the school to find out. He would really go off if he thought she was checking on him. She thought, *if he does go to school and acts weird, maybe they'll have him arrested. Then, I can get him back to the hospital.*

She enjoyed being with her students that day. Their enthusiasm was contagious, and she completely threw herself into teaching. By the end of the day, she felt stronger and renewed.

CHAPTER 86

Bill decided not to try and catch Elizabeth at the daycare that morning. He knew she would take Angela to daycare and then go to school. He wanted to wait until she picked up Angela and then he would follow her to wherever she was living. He knew that was going to be the only way he would be try to catch her with Luke.

He got ready to go to school. He was almost out of the door when he decided that he didn't need to go to work anymore. *No point in going to work! I'm not going to be around to spend the money!* He called in and requested a substitute so that no one would question his absence.

That afternoon, Bill parked the truck on a street a couple of blocks away from the daycare center. He walked to a spot across the street from the daycare and stood behind some bushes. He saw Elizabeth get out of the car and he jumped out onto the sidewalk. He wasn't able to control himself long enough for her to go in and come back out with Angela so that he could follow them.

"Come home. Stop acting like a bitch! If you come back now, I'll let you live. If you don't, you and Angela are both dead."

Elizabeth screamed, "Leave me alone! I'm calling the police! You stay away from me and Angela!" She ran to the daycare and didn't look back.

Mary held the door open for her and then locked it behind her. She called out, "Code Red!" Her assistant helped the children go up the stairs into the hallway. Mary called the police and told them that Bill was there and was dangerous.

Angela ran to Elizabeth when she came in. She heard everything Mary told the police about Bill. Instead of going upstairs with the other children for the Code Red, she hid under Mary's desk to stay close to Elizabeth.

Elizabeth watched Bill disappear around the corner. When she was sure that he wasn't going to try to get in the daycare, she crawled under the desk with Angela. Because Angela was trembling and crying, she cuddled Angela in her arms. "*Shhh*, it's okay. Don't you worry. Nothing bad is going to happen. The nice policeman who is coming to help us won't let it."

"I'm scared. Daddy might get me and Bearie." Elizabeth's heart was breaking because Angela was so scared, and she couldn't comfort her.

When the policeman arrived, Elizabeth and Mary told him what happened. The officer was sympathetic but said he couldn't help them.

"He stayed at least 100 feet away from you. Stalking isn't against the law, but it should be. You can swear out a warrant for his arrest because he's been ordered to leave the house. I need to tell you that judges rarely act on those requests if the battered spouse isn't living in the house and in immediate danger. I can't do anything about him following you as long as he keeps his distance. I'm so sorry."

"Going back to the house is not an option. He'll just get back in and then he'll kill me. At least, now, he doesn't know where we live."

"Do you want me to go to your house and say something to him? Maybe I can scare him into leaving you alone."

"No, please don't do that. He's psychotic and won't listen to reason. If you go there, it would just enrage him more. He's so crazy that he might try to shoot you when you get out of the car. It's better to just leave him alone."

"I'll walk you to the car in case he's still out there. Then I'll drive around the block to make sure he left." Elizabeth thanked him and picked up Angela to carry her to the car.

Mary watched them walk to the car. Her intuition told her that this was not going to end well at all. She had never seen anyone look as crazy as Bill when he screamed at Elizabeth from across the street. She called Henry and asked him to come to the daycare center, just in case Bill came back.

After Elizabeth and Angela were safe in the car, the officer left. She drove around for twenty minutes and to see if Bill was following her. She didn't see his truck, so she finally drove back to Carolyn's. Bill went straight home after his encounter with Elizabeth. He decided that he didn't care where she stayed. Killing Luke wasn't as important as killing Elizabeth and Angela. He knew for sure that she was taking Angela to daycare now and he was going to get them the next day.

Chapter 87

That night, he descended into complete madness. Although he was in the grips of the deepest depression imaginable, he was euphoric because his pain would soon be over. Elizabeth and Angela were going to die and he relished the idea of killing them. He was going to kill Angela first and watch Elizabeth squirm, knowing she was next. Once he killed them, he would be able to kill himself and end his pain forever.

He imagined the headlines in the newspaper: <u>Outstanding Teacher Driven To Suicide By His Cheating Wife.</u> Nowhere in the headlines, he imagined, did he come across as a bad guy. In fact, in his mind, he was a hero. He was certain everyone would understand that he had been forced to do it.

He had never felt so alive in his life and everything in the house seemed to be shimmering. He pulled everything out of the refrigerator and threw it in the trash. Then, he dumped everything out of the cabinets because he wasn't going to need food anymore. He went to the garage and brought in a ten-gallon can of gasoline. He wasn't going to need a house either.

It's a shame that I'm going to be dead and won't get to read the sensational headlines. So many people will come to my funeral. Students, teachers, and people I don't even know will come and pay their respects. They'll look sadly down at me in my coffin and say how sad it is that she drove me to suicide. They'll know that she got what she deserved. Tomorrow is going to be a glorious day!

CHAPTER 88

Elizabeth was really shaken up by the scene at the daycare. She paced around the basement long after Laura and Angela were asleep. Although he had been across the street, she saw the madness in his eyes. *I know, beyond any doubt, that he's completely insane and there's no hope that I can reason with him. Even if I get him into a hospital, he'll get out, go off the medicine, and come after us again. The police can't protect us and it's just a matter of time until he finds out where we're living. Everyone around us is in real danger. Maybe I can take Angela to live in another state. I could change my name, but he would just track us down through my social security number. Maybe I can send Angela to live with our cousin, Wanda, for a while. I need to stay here where I have a job and know people who can help me. I've never felt so lost or alone.*

She went into the tiny bathroom, shut the door, then got on her knees and prayed. "Please, God, help me. I don't know what to do. He's so sick and I can't help him. Please touch his heart and mind and make him well enough to know that he has to take the medicine. I'm so afraid he's going to hurt someone or himself if he doesn't get back on the medicine. Please, dear Lord, protect Angela and keep her safe. She's just a baby with her life ahead of her. Dear God, please protect everyone around me and don't let Bill hurt them. Forgive me for my sins, I've tried to be a good person and I know that I've fallen short at times. I'm truly sorry and beg your forgiveness. Give me the strength to go on and to face what's coming." Then she recited the 23rd Psalm.

The Lord is my shepherd; I shall not want. He maketh me to lie down in green pastures: he leadeth me beside the still waters. He restoreth my soul: he leadeth me in the paths of righteousness for his name's sake. Yea, though I walk through the valley of the shadow of death, I will fear no evil: for thou art with me; thy rod and thy staff comfort me. Thou preparest a table before me in the presence of mine enemies: thou anointest my head with oil; my cup runneth over. Surely goodness and mercy will follow me all the days of my life: and I will dwell in the house of the Lord forever. Amen.

She stayed on her knees for several minutes in the quiet bathroom. She was trying to hear God, if he spoke to her. Her knees hurt, but she waited and listened. She finally stood up. As she stood up, she could hear Elvis singing *You'll Never Walk Alone* in her head. She looked up and said, "Thank you, God." Elizabeth knew that she wasn't alone in that tiny bathroom that night.

CHAPTER 89

Exhaustion caught up with her and she needed to get a few hours of sleep. She decided to take Angela to daycare early to avoid Bill. If she could avoid him tomorrow, maybe she and Laura could think of something to get out of this mess. She looked at the clock and saw that it was three in the morning. She set the alarm for five and snuggled close to Angela.

She quickly fell asleep. She dreamed that she and Angela were swinging in the park. Angela was giggling and her laughter made Elizabeth happy. They were swinging high up in the air when the alarm went off. Fragments of her dream stayed with her for a few seconds and she was happy for those few seconds. Reality quickly set in as she realized that they were still in Carolyn's basement. The alarm woke up Angela and Laura, too. Elizabeth helped Angela to get dressed as she told Laura that she was going to leave an hour early in case Bill was waiting for her at the daycare. Laura agreed that it was a smart thing to do. Laura went upstairs and brought back two steaming mugs of coffee. Elizabeth quickly drank her coffee and finished getting ready. Laura turned on the TV for Angela to watch while she and Elizabeth talked.

Elizabeth spoke quietly so that Angela couldn't hear what she said, "We can't keep living like this. I tried to think of what to do last night while you were asleep, but I couldn't come up with anything except running away and changing my name. Bill's not going to stop until he kills me, but I have to protect Angela. Maybe I should send Angela to live with Wanda until this is over. Her kids are about the same age as Angela and she would be happy there for a while. But Bill might find out where she is and go to get her. I just don't know what to do. Try to come up with something today, if you can."

Laura's eyes welled with tears, "I'll figure something out. You be careful today. I love you." That was the first time Laura cried throughout the whole ordeal.

Chapter 90

Bill didn't sleep after he brought the gasoline into the house. He cleaned his guns and loaded the clips. He took the guns and extra bullets to the truck. He went back into the house and slashed Angela's bed. He piled her blankets in the middle of the hallway, gathered all of the pillows in the house and threw them onto the pile of blankets. He went to the garage and found an old, rusty axe. He used the axe to chop up the coffee table, and he threw the pieces of it on the pile in the hallway. By the time he was done, he had assembled enough items to make a great bon fire.

He took a shower and wore his favorite shirt. He paced back and forth in the living room and waited until it was time to go to the daycare center. He wanted to get there early to be able to catch Elizabeth and Angela before they went in. He set the alarm just in case he fell asleep. The alarm went off at five, but he was awake and ready to go when it buzzed. He had never felt so alive and focused.

He poured the gasoline over the pile in the hallway and threw a match on it. He watched the flames dance and listened to the screaming smoke alarm. He laughed as he casually walked out of the back door and got into his truck. By the time he pulled out of the driveway, black smoke was billowing out of the house. He didn't care! He didn't need the house anymore!

CHAPTER 91

When Elizabeth got to the daycare center, she quickly took Angela out of the car, picked her up, and ran to the door. She was out of breath when she put Angela on the floor inside the daycare. Mary could see that Elizabeth was terrified and she instinctively hugged her. "You're okay. He's not out there. I've been watching the street. Try to calm down."

Elizabeth tried to slow her breathing, but it took a couple of minutes before she got it under control. She reached down to remove Angela's coat and saw that Angela looked scared to death. Elizabeth picked her up and carried her into the playroom. She squatted down so that she was eye level with Angela.

"You're safe here with Miss Mary. Mommy made sure of it. You don't need to worry about anything. Nothing bad is going to happen to you. You're my precious baby and I love you."

"I love you, too, Mommy."

Elizabeth hugged Angela tightly and kissed her goodbye. She thanked Mary again for all her help and support. She looked up and down the street before she ran to her car. He wasn't out there.

CHAPTER 92

Elizabeth got all the way to the door of her car before she saw Bill's truck coming around the corner. Thankfully, she had left the keys in the ignition when she took Angela into the daycare. She turned the key and the engine started just as his truck slammed into the rear of her car. Mary saw Bill's truck ram into Elizabeth's car, screamed Code Red, and ran to call the police. Elizabeth was halfway down the block by the time Mary reached the phone.

When Bill's truck rammed her car, she jerked the gearshift handle into drive and stomped on the gas. She was going fifty miles an hour down the narrow street, but he was right on her tail. Her only hope was to get to the freeway and lose him in the traffic. She turned a corner too fast and her car fishtailed. She was able to get it under control but barely avoided crashing into an oncoming car. Her rear window exploded. *Oh God, he's shooting at me!*

Elizabeth held the gas pedal all the way down on the floor. She drove around two cars stopped at the red light, and was lucky that no cars were crossing the intersection when she sped through. Bill followed right behind her. She was going so fast that she missed the turn to the freeway. She took the next right and then the next left in an effort to lose him. Turn after turn, he stayed right on her bumper. She knew he was still shooting at her car, but she didn't dare take her eyes off the road in front of her.

Elizabeth hoped that she would pass a patrol car, but the residential streets were deserted. She had taken so many turns that she didn't recognize the area. She knew she must be in the back of one of the older subdivisions of Louisville. She drove so fast that she couldn't read the street signs. She was hopelessly lost, but she kept driving as she tried to get away from him. Elizabeth took another right and immediately realized that she had made a fatal mistake. The street ended about a block away. Big, brick houses lined the horseshoe-shaped court. She knew she was trapped!

CHAPTER 93

Elizabeth was in a blind panic. She was breathing hard--almost panting--but she couldn't seem to get enough air into her lungs. Just before she came to the end of the court, she slammed on the breaks. The car skidded sideways and came to a stop. She looked around and knew there was no way to drive around Bill's truck. His arm was out of the window and he was still shooting. If she tried to drive past the truck, he would have a straight shot at her head. He shot so much that it sounded like a war zone. A thought raced through her mind. *Maybe he'll run out of bullets.* She heard a bullet whiz past her head and watched the front windshield shatter.

She ducked down and crawled across the seat to the passenger door. As she lay flat on the seat, she reached for the door handle while bullets flew above her head. Her hand found the handle. She pulled it down and pushed out as hard as she could. When she felt the door open, she scrambled out, staggered to her feet and started running. She was trying to make it to the back of the house which stood in front of her.

She glanced back. Bill had pulled his truck up against the car and he was getting out. He had a shotgun in his hands. It wasn't the gun he had been shooting because that gun had fit in his hand. She wondered how she had noticed that. She realized she was seeing everything in slow motion. She could see each blade of grass in the lawn as she tried to run for her life. She had taken a couple of steps when she felt a sharp pain in her back and fell to her knees.

Angela's sweet, newborn face appeared before her. She saw her mother and father kissing under the mistletoe. She saw Laura drinking a glass of wine and laughing. Angela's face appeared again. However, this time, Angela looked like she did this morning when Elizabeth left her at the daycare. She was trying to get to her feet when she heard another loud explosion. She fell face forward onto the grass. Elizabeth didn't feel any pain, but she knew that her time on this earth was over because she was floating toward a beautiful, bright, white light.

CHAPTER 94

Bill knew he had hit Elizabeth when he saw her fall to her knees. *I got her now!* He took two more steps and shot again. He saw her fall forward onto the grass and she wasn't moving. Bill ran over to her body, bent down, and rolled her over. Her eyes were open and staring at the sky, but he knew that she wasn't seeing anything. She was dead. *I don't give a damn if she is dead. She still has that beautiful face. No one will ever see your beautiful face again!* He held the barrel of the gun about two inches from her face and shot again. Her beautiful face was gone. *You still have that beautiful body. I'll take care of that!* He put the barrel on her chest and pulled the trigger.

He heard sirens. *Somebody has already called the cops. I won't be able to go back for Angela. That's okay. Killing Elizabeth is good enough. The cops don't need to hurry. I'll be dead long before they get here.* He pointed the gun at the side of his head and pulled the trigger. His world went black and his body fell on top of Elizabeth.

CHAPTER 95

When the police and ambulance arrived a few minutes later, Bill was still alive. The gun's recoil had affected his shot.

The police officer pulled Bill's wallet from his pocket and looked at his driver's license as the paramedics put him onto a stretcher. He handed the license to one of the paramedics and grimly said, "Get him to the hospital!"

The ambulance raced through the streets to University Hospital. In the ambulance, the paramedics worked frantically to put in an IV and used a hand respirator to keep him breathing. By the time they arrived at the emergency room, a team of surgeons had already been assembled in the OR. The paramedics ran as they pushed the gurney through the hallways and into the OR. Bill's brain matter and blood leaked onto the gurney as they ran. He was brain dead, but they kept him alive because he had signed on his license to be an organ donor.

Because of the heroic measures taken by the paramedics, Bill's organs were still viable. His eyes gave sight to a blind child. His heart, liver, and kidneys saved dying patients. His skin was removed from his body and sent to burns hospitals to be used as grafts. More than a dozen patients were helped or saved by Bill's organs.

CHAPTER 96

Donna was asleep when Ed awoke at six on Wednesday morning. He went into the kitchen, started the coffee, and went to the front door to get the newspaper. When he opened the door and bent down to pick up the paper, he recognized the two pictures that stared up at him from the front page. "Oh, my God!"

He went into the kitchen and poured a cup of coffee for Donna. He walked into the bedroom and put the cup on the nightstand beside the bed. Ed gently shook her shoulder, "Donna, wake up." She opened her eyes and saw the look on his face.

"What's wrong!?"

Ed just said, "Sit up and take a drink of coffee before the phone rings."

Donna couldn't understand what he was talking about until she looked at the paper in his hand. She saw the photos of Elizabeth and Bill and cried out, "Oh, God! No! He killed her!" As Donna reached for the paper, the phone rang. It was Laura calling.

EPILOGUE

The crowd at Elizabeth's funeral overflowed into the parking lot. In addition to her family and friends, the Mayor of Louisville, the Superintendent of Jefferson County Schools, teachers and students from her school, Roxanne, Mary, Henry, Carolyn, and many others who knew her attended. Local, state, and national news people were there to cover her story. Elizabeth's blue coffin was closed and a picture of Angela sat on top of the coffin next to a blanket of white carnations. When Elizabeth's coffin was taken to the cemetery, the cars following the hearse stretched for more than a mile. People stood on the side of the road that lead to the cemetery and held candles. Metro police estimated that more than a thousand people paid tribute to Elizabeth that day. In lieu of flowers, her family asked that donations be given to the women's shelter.

Bill's funeral was held the day after Elizabeth's. The only people who attended were his parents, brother, sister, and Larry. The media didn't cover his funeral but chose, instead, to run stories which described him as a murderous psychotic.

They also ran stories about the shelter which had protected Elizabeth in her time of need. Donations poured into the shelter because of the stories. In her memory, Elizabeth's art students went to the shelter and painted a mural on the courtyard wall. Many of them volunteered to continue the art therapy for the children.

The school where Elizabeth taught placed a plaque on the wall in memory of her. Mary planted a Dogwood tree in the yard of the daycare center and placed a plaque at its base in memory of Elizabeth.

Gary visited Elizabeth's grave a few days after her funeral and told her that he was sorry he had ever let her go.

Donna deeply mourned the loss of her dear friend. She told Ed that the picture of the orange lilies that Elizabeth had painted for her would forever symbolize Elizabeth's life. She was a bright flower in the world and the black background of the painting represented the darkness that she had endured during her last days on earth.

Luke saw the report about Elizabeth on national TV news. He sent a donation to a local women's shelter in honor of Elizabeth.

****

Angela wanted to keep Elizabeth's nightgown because it smelled like her mommy. Laura put it in a sealed, plastic bag to keep the scent from fading. As she grew up, anytime Angela was upset, she opened the bag and was comforted by her mother's scent. She slept with Bearie until she went to college.

Laura adopted Angela and raised her to be a strong woman.

AFTERWARD

Orange lilies grow wild along Kentucky's country roads. We enjoy their beauty as we drive past them and we don't give them much more thought. It occurred to me, as I thought about a title for this book, that abused women and children are everywhere just like the wild, orange lilies. We know they exist, but we don't give them much thought unless the headlines of the day tell another tragic story about them.

Women's shelters are overcrowded and have limited funding. I hope that this book will bring a new focus to the need that exists to help abused women and children. Please take time to find out about shelters in your area and do whatever you can to support them.

If you need help or if you know someone who needs help, please call the National Domestic Abuse Hotline. 1-800-799-SAFE (7233). They can give you information about shelter locations, state laws that protect people in abusive situations, and abuse counselors in your area. Their help is always anonymous and confidential and the helpline is open 24 hours a day, 7 days a week.